DAN  HANLY

To Josh
I Hope you enjoy!

THE
GREAT
LEAP

CHILDREN OF INAURON:
BOOK 1

Copyright © 2024 Dan Hanly

All rights reserved

The characters and events portrayed in this book are fictitious. Any similarity to real persons, living or dead, is coincidental and not intended by the author.

No part of this book may be reproduced, or stored in a retrieval system, or transmitted in any form or by any means, electronic, mechanical, photocopying, recording, or otherwise, without express written permission of the publisher.

Cover design by: GetCovers.com

*To my wife, for her unwavering support, and to
all the others that encouraged me along the way.*

CONTENTS

Copyright

Dedication

Title Page

Prologue	1
1	10
2	29
3	40
4	47
5	54
6	68
7	84
8	96
9	100
10	109
11	117
12	126
13	136

14	148
15	161
16	176
17	186
18	194
19	207
20	217
21	229
22	240
23	253
24	265
25	275
26	295
27	304
Epilogue	311
Afterword	323
Join The Children Of Inauron	325
About The Author	329

THE GREAT LEAP

Children of Inauron: Book 1

DAN HANLY

PROLOGUE

The ringing in her ears would not stop.

There she stood, unblinking. The chaotic scene in front of her played out in perfect detail on her glassy, deep-set eyes. The inferno blazed, and like a swarm of locusts, the townspeople descended upon it with buckets of water from the well. The marshal screamed orders over the roar of the fire, mothers yelled for their children, water loudly sizzled as it doused small parts of the blaze. She could see nor hear any of it, for her mind and her senses were not under her control.

The darkness of the night was illuminated almost entirely by the flames.

The Sanctuary burned.

The Sanctuary of Inauron was the focal point of their entire lives; it was the centre of their town Penny Grove, their religious centre, trade-centre and school; nary an activity was conducted in the Grove without some part of it being managed within the doors of that circular, domed stone building.

And now the blaze consumed it, and she could do naught but stare in horror as she was wrenched away to a more comfortable place; a calming place, a place of beauty and wonder. She was often brought to these places, whenever hardship bubbled up around her, it was her survival mechanism. Despite her eyes being fixated on the fire, she could still picture the gorgeous rolling hills, long grass swaying in the wind flurries, the sun, cool but bright. The incessant ringing in her ears worked hard to bury the sounds of the desperate rush of the townsfolk. Her body and mind were working in tandem to force her away from their terrifying reality.

Growing up in Penny Grove had not granted Fleta Timber the same experience as that of her peers. Her entire sixteen years of life were filled with pain, anger and torment. She had nothing that was wholly hers; her life decisions were made for her, she had no possessions to speak of, even the clothes on her back were provided for her, by others in the town, as acts of charity. Her family were at the bottom of a long pecking-order within the Grove, so much that they were almost on the verge of destitution. Her parents couldn't allow her to culture her own life because she was needed to help them support theirs. On top of all this, her bodily autonomy was torn from her regularly, on a whim, by her cruel Uncle, the very person charged with her care whilst her parents worked to provide for them.

The entrancing fires did not furnish her with the same sense of loss that many of the townspeople were feeling. For her, the fires represented change. She could hopefully, finally, emerge from these fires with a new sense of purpose, a new mission, one that she alone could control. As resolute as she felt, there was still a raw terror that gripped her - was the terror just a natural response to change, or something more? Just as a toddler who learned to walk unaided, she knew the path ahead would be fraught with dangers, but she would emerge with a new sense of freedom that only she would oversee.

"Flea!"

Her brother's pet name for her, screamed in her face, snapped her back to Penny Grove. As the sunlit hills faded, and the thick, orange-tinted, smoke-shrouded night revealed itself once more, she saw her twin, Bronson, in front of her reaching out to shake her from her fantasy.

She held a hand out and recoiled in anticipation of his touch.

"Why are you just standing there?" He paused, "did you get it?"

She nodded.

"Well, where is it?"

"Not there."

Bronson buried his head in his hands.

"What are we going to do?"

She blinked for the first time in far too long, her eyes stung from the smoke as rivulets of tears drew a path through her soot stained cheeks revealing the paleness of her skin beneath. Fleta shrugged without turning to face her twin, eyes still transfixed by the raging fire.

"Wait," he noticed, "you changed your clothes?"

"They're sending us all to die in the Wildlands, Bronson. None of it matters anymore."

The council had met under an emergency session the moment it was revealed that their group of friends, ten in all, were present in The Sanctuary when the blaze began. The council of elders were not young or fit enough to help with the fire-fighting, so they did what they always do; assign blame, behind the scenes. They were not interested in an investigation nor evidence of culpability; they wanted nothing more than to justify their own existence by enacting punishment and controlling the citizenry's perception of the evening.

Six of their eight friends that had

accompanied Fleta and Bronson into The Sanctuary that evening were tied together, kneeling in the mud alongside the tavern. Their faces were lit by the fire and their eyes danced around with the flames, but they were expressionless.

Lawson's face was bruised and his lip swollen; he'd put up a fight, but after the guards had subdued him, his closest friends, Wendy, Piper and Stokely came quietly. Kenley had tried to run, but his own father, a renowned hunter, found him and brought him back to the tavern to face justice. Corin, who was in training to become a Devoted at the Sanctuary, prostrated herself in front of her beloved place of worship as it burned and, despite her normally passive demeanour, she had caused the guards quite the struggle in arresting her. Two guards appeared from behind the tavern, bringing with them Addison and Dawn; the betrothed couple had clasped hands with each other and wouldn't allow the guards to separate them, not wanting a fight, the guards simply tied them together, and pushed them down into the mud. Eight captured, two to go. Fleta knew that her and her brother were next to be captured.

"Let's go," Bronson said, panicked, "let's leave now."

"What's the point," she said.

"They'll arrest us."

"Let them."

Bronson frowned and reached for her hand, but she snatched it away

Fleta knew that banishment was her only recourse in this life. She wanted out of Penny Grove; she wanted out of the life she hated. If she left without being compelled, she would feel responsible for her parent's eventual fate, and she couldn't live on-the-run as Bronson seemed to suggest. She would accept this punishment because it offered her the only guilt-free, viable method of leaving for good.

"Fleta please," he said, using her full name - he rarely did. "I can't do this."

"They're going to catch us. You know that. It's easier if we just hand ourselves in."

"They won't, I swear to you."

"You can't swear, 'cos you can't know," she quipped, turning away from him towards the tavern.

His lips tightened, and he exhaled through his nose.

"I'll take you with me whether or not you want to go," he spat; yet another person vowing to wrest control of her life away from her. She wouldn't allow it. Without responding, she simply started walking across the town-centre, towards the tavern.

"Wait," he cried.

She didn't wait. Her despondency was in control of her now, and she could not stop her advance, she saw no point, no reason to stay, and no reason to fight.

Her boots made a suckering sound with each step as she crossed the muddy town centre. Too many spilled buckets of water from the fire fighting had turned the ground swamp-like. Each step bore the risk of slippage, but she pushed through fixated on the side of tavern and her captured peers.

Bronson was not so successful; he slid across the mud, clashing with fire-fighting townspeople and wailing spectators as he tried to catch up to her. A man threw him to the ground as they made contact, splattering mud on one half of his face. Without so much of a thought for his own safety, he scrambled back to his feet quickly to chase after her.

As he reached her, he grasped one of her forearms, but it was too late, a guard had already grabbed the other.

"Well that was easy," the guard said. Fleta saw anger flash momentarily in the guard's expression. These guards were the same ones that had protected them as they grew up, but these were not the friendly expressive faces she was used to seeing patrolling around the town.

Bronson clenched his teeth, released Fleta's arm and turned to run, but he was too late, another guard had him by the shoulders.

"Oh, no you don't," the second guard said through clenched teeth.

"We had nothing to do with the fire," he screamed.

"Yep, yep," the guard said, then feigned a laugh to the other, "looks like another one is innocent."

Bronson was tied with rope and pushed down into the mud alongside Dawn. The pair shared a sympathetic glance. Bronson placed his head in his lap, hiding from the world as he was wont to do.

Fleta held her clenched fists out, knuckles pointed upwards, and as she did, she noticed something that chilled her to the bone. Before she could consider it, a rope was tied around them and she was pushed to the mud next to her brother.

She felt as though her consciousness was elsewhere, and she acted almost entirely without forethought. She tried to drift to her rolling hills once more to calm her rising panic, but she wasn't able to remain; what she had noticed whilst being bound by the guards birthed an uncomfortable worry that kept her from retreating, a thought that slowly bubbled up within her and began to dominate her consciousness.

She had noticed her hands.

Hands she had forgotten to clean whilst she changed her clothes.

She hoped and hoped to Inauron that nobody could see the sticky, drying blood that covered them.

As she settled onto the ground, she opened her hands and pressed them into the slick, soft mud, masking what she'd done.

1

Into the Wildlands

Haggard and dishevelled, they marched through the night. The cold winds between the dense trees chilled them to the bone; they were not adequately dressed or prepared for this trek. Owls hooted, crows cawed, and bats flittered between the branches. The only sounds that pierced the cold night were the cracking of sticks and rustling of leaves beneath their feet, interspersed with the breaths of the ten; some light, some heavy, some strained.

This place in which they walked was primaeval, an ancient forest that had formed along with the land itself; it covered the entire southern area of the continent as if it were the wild, unkempt beard on the face of the world.

With their backs to civilisation, they walked further into the uncharted expanse of the

Wildlands. There was a wetness to the air, a cold humidity that carried the stench of decomposing foliage that littered the woodland floor like a soft carpet of mulch. Water dripped from the trees in large globules as the region's fine rain collected in the leafy canopy. Their hair had matted to their scalps, and the heat created by their bodies beneath their layers smelled of mildew and body odour.

They had been quietly instructed to follow the river to the lake at the heart of the Wildlands, but the way the small river meandered and dipped in and out of small hills made it difficult to know whether or not they remained on their planned path. In parts, the water gushed over the rocks; in others, it was barely a trickle in defiance of their expectations. It flowed at varying speeds and currents, and the group often wondered whether they were following the correct river or even the same river as before.

The water was as clear as they'd ever seen, almost liquid flowing glass, barely discernible if not for the rush betraying its shape. The sound of the river would have been pleasant if not for the seriousness of their journey - they had no time to take in the sights and absorb the sounds of this place. Each of the ten broken souls had their minds elsewhere, thinking deeply, lamenting, planning or even grieving.

They trudged on, not one word spoken

between them. The group found paths in the mere suggestion of walkways favoured by the game of the woods, ways that took them down steep inclines slick with mud and dense with shrubbery. They passed fallen trees laden with yellowing layered fungi, saw plants of varieties not found near their homes, heard the call of birds they were unfamiliar with, and rustling in the bushes that unnerved them. Everything about their surroundings made them realise how little of this world they had experienced.

Despite the tension between them, they helped each other over rocks and held out arms to support each other as the terrain became more unforgiving. They walked along a trail that sloped high above the trickling brook many feet below. A steep bank dropped from within a handspan of the path to the bottom. A fall down this bank would be fatal with a surface littered with rocks, scree, and the sharp protruding wood of fallen trees. They stepped gingerly away from the precipice as they moved over the path. A tree previously rooted had fallen down the bank, pulling much of the pathway with it, making an already precarious walkway even more so.

One of the youngest in the group, Stokely, a meek, pallid boy of around fifteen years, slipped and fell to one knee; his other dangled out over the edge and kicked out quickly as he scrambled backwards; he panted as he struggled back to his feet, mud and detritus staining his knees and boots. Stones and dirt clods escaped from his flailing leg and bounced down the sheer bank to the river below.

"Rest," he gasped, "I need rest."

Addison, a gangly redhead, one of the eldest of the group just shy of twenty summers, looked to the sky at the ailing light between the trees, a black backlit gauze of interlocked branches. He pushed his matted red hair from his face. They'd been walking for almost an entire day and stopped only twice in the intervening time, but he knew that without rest, they wouldn't get much farther.

"Let's find somewhere flat," he said monotonously, closing his eyes in a laboured blink, exhaling slowly.

"We passed a small grassy clearing about five or ten minutes ago," Dawn whispered to Addison, her hand still clenching his as it had most of the journey. Addison nodded and began to double back. The group followed.

Lawson, another of the elders of the group, a dark-haired, blue-eyed boy of middling stature, held out an arm for Stokely to grasp onto, supporting him as he properly regained his footing. Looking down, Lawson could see the slip-marks made by Stokely's boots in the mud; it would have been a dangerous fall.

When they arrived, the clearing greeted them with a beautiful, soft, inviting carpet of grass spread out in a small field, a blemish on the otherwise constant landscape of trees around them. Upon entering from the tree line, one by one, the group slowly dispersed and began to halt their movements for the first time in far too many hours. The gentle dusting of fine evening rain cooling them.

The grey sky above them was now textured instead of the smooth monochrome spread they'd been used to seeing between the leaves. There was a pinkness to some of the clouds as the setting sun had caught their undersides. The rain was finally beginning to abate, giving way to a cool breeze that caressed the reddened faces of the group. Light levels had lowered, which drew long ominous shadows across the clearing, and the bats which had previously stayed beneath the dark canopy of the forest began to dance across the open sky above them.

Addison threw down the large stick he had been using as a make-shift walking aid; he let go of Dawn's hand and swept both of his through his hair, then across his face from his nose and eyes to his cheeks, willing the colour back into his features. Dawn fell to her knees beside him and beckoned for him to join her; he did so with ease, his feet and legs desperate for respite.

Fleta pointed to a spot near the edge of the

clearing, away from the others, and her twin brother Bronson threw their small pack down onto it. They didn't have much in terms of supplies; some dried salted meat, water skins, and a change of clothes each. They weren't given much time to prepare for this journey, exiled as they were from their homes. Fleta was sure the others had more with them, but she had other business to attend to after the verdict was handed down; she eyed the crusted blood beneath her fingernails with disgust.

She stood with her arms outstretched; her face pointed to the sky. Her darkened deep-set eyes closed slowly, hiding behind them the intense blueness of her irises, taking in the coolness and moistness of the air around her. Her dirty dark-coloured hair was knotted and unruly, and she did what she could to pull it back and out of her face whilst she enjoyed the remnants of the rain. She moved her small cracked lips around willing them back to life.

Fleta was adorned in much the same attire as the rest of the group albeit with a noticeable lack of quality in her hand-me-down garment. She wore a dark-green coloured gown that fell almost to the ground, styled to cinch in at the waist. The gown was long-sleeved, keeping her covered enough from the cold during their trek, but one thing that nobody had ever explained to her, was that a gown like this gets ever heavier with the rain. Decorated with black and turquoise banding around her waist, sleeves and cuffs, her dress looked like it had been somebody's show-piece, once upon a time; now however, after repairs and patches, the dress had lost its previous glamour. It didn't even fit snugly; the sleeves were too long. Whoever had originally purchased or tailored this dress, evidently had a different body shape to the petite-framed Fleta. Her mother's beaded necklace was the only jewellery she wore; a memento from a grieving parent who couldn't even look her in the eyes.

The others fell weary. One by one, they all took to the ground allowing the long grass to envelop them like a soft mattress. Wendy and Piper, who had been joined at the hip this entire journey, sat near the base of an old tree; Wendy's previously perfect, straight black hair was partially frayed from the wind and matted with the wetness from the damp air; gone was her usual royal-like appearance, replaced with a drawn and exhausted visage. Kenley sat himself down near Addison. A little over two years younger than him, Kenley spent a great deal of time looking up to Addison and so it was only natural for him to sleep near the person he felt most comfortable with. Despite their shared predicament, it was clear to Fleta that existing alliances would remain strong.

Lawson threw his pack onto the ground and lay back upon it, arms behind his head, with his outstretched legs resting on one another casually. Stokely brushed off the mud and leaves from his knees and sank into the soft grass near Lawson. Corin, the most devout of the group, prostrated herself on the ground, knees tucked beneath her, forehead almost touching the green blades; hands clasped in prayer.

Bronson moved closer to his sister. "Are you okay?" he asked quietly.

"Yeah," she lied, "just perfect."

She voluntarily collapsed onto the soft carpet of the clearing, her brother following suit. She placed her head on their pack, and Bronson did the same. They lay ear to ear, with their bodies facing opposite directions.

"You seem quiet," Bronson said.

"Well, we've just been kicked out of our homes," she replied.

"You hated it there," he whispered, then, after a pause, "thought you'd be happy."

This irked her, but she wasn't able to communicate why. She did hate it there... she hated everything about her childhood; their absent parents, terrifying uncle, and drug-addicted twin brother. She should have been happier than she was to have left for good. Maybe it was the circumstances of their exile; she'd not left of her own accord, and she'd not decided to walk, instead, they'd been ousted.

A small fire was all it took... and before they knew it, the whole Sanctuary was ablaze. It wasn't her fire; she hadn't started it nor been involved. This entire situation was another example of her powerlessness in the face of her ever-turbulent fate.

"I'm just thinking about what comes next," she said. "You're going to get sick."

Bronson closed his eyes at this and exhaled through his nose lightly. His uncle had him addicted to gravel a few years ago, and since then, her brother's life had inadvertently revolved around where he could get his next fix. He'd stopped caring about her, stopped working towards his future. His single-mindedness to getting his fix was all he had; and now, it was over.

"I wish you'd been able to get some for me," he whispered.

"He wouldn't give it to me, you know this," she said firmly.

"I know," he turned his head on their pack to face her, and she did the same; they looked into each other's eyes like they did when they were children. "I don't blame you for it, but I still wish I had some to wean myself off it slowly. Now I'm going to withdraw and it's going to be tough."

She loved her brother, but this was a bed of his own making. Before the fire, they'd never addressed his addiction openly, but they both knew what was happening to him. She had her own issues to deal with and hadn't the energy to rescue her brother - a brother who she was sure would insist he didn't need rescuing. They had no idea how to talk about such an emotionally charged topic; bringing it up in the wrong way could sever their already tenuous relationship. She placed a cold hand on his cheek, feeling the warmth radiate from his skin, and her eyebrows lifted in sympathy.

Nearby, Dawn asked Addison, her betrothed, to pray with her. Others in the group heard it too, and each began to rouse themselves enough to join the ritual they'd engaged in daily for as long as they could remember. Corin lifted herself off the grass and sat on her knees with her hands clasped neatly in her lap. Dawn nodded to Corin to start the prayer.

"Inauron," Corin began. A few in the group followed their lead and took to their knees in respect. The others, where exhaustion was too intense, closed their eyes from where they lay.

"He who gave us strength," Dawn said, leading the next passage for herself. Quietly and slowly she spoke, feeling every word as it left her lips, "To fight for our lives,"

Most of the group prayed aloud with them.

Addison lowered his gaze but was otherwise unmoved by the show of spirituality of the surrounding group. He mouthed the words along with her, in respect of the beliefs of the others, if not his own.

"To open the doors, which others had closed." Corin continued the alternation of the prayer with Dawn; the awkward harmony of mumbles from the others in the group soon began to slot into place, morphing the sounds from a discordant din into a deep, enchanting drone.

To her dismay, Fleta found herself becoming moved by the prayer. There was something peaceful and heartfelt about it. She'd been saying this prayer by rote for much of her life, but this time, in light of their circumstances, being exiled from their homes, combined with the exhaustion and the sense of awkward kinship they each felt, she received the prayer in a way she never had before. She closed her eyes, and as the words continued, she felt a light shiver down her spine and into her kidneys. She felt blood rushing to her extremities, warming them for the first time that day.

"He who fortified our resolve, amid our pain, and sacrificed himself to push us forth."

"Upon these knees do we giveth thanks; upon these knees do we ask for strength," Corin chanted. As a tear ran down Dawn's cheek, Addison lifted a thumb to wipe her eye gently.

Even he felt on the verge of breaking down, so moved by this experience. Dawn's voice began to undulate with her emotions as she finished the prayer, "upon these knees do we giveth honour; upon these knees do we ask for a path."

As the prayer finished, they each began to open their eyes and sit back on their feet, some falling back to the grassy carpet of the clearing. Dawn fell forward into Addison's arms, and he held her close as she grieved her loss, the same loss suffered by them all.

It wasn't a person they all grieved for, but a town, a life, a future, a family, one that was stolen from them by the cruel flames of fate.

They'd been away from the town for nearly a day, but Fleta and Bronson still bore the stain of soot upon their faces, hands and beneath their fingernails. Fleta's tears had cleaned the soot from her skin, leaving rivulets from her eyes to her chin. Bronson put an arm around his sister and held her close, but her thoughts drifted, and energy drained from her, removing her ability to stay focused on the warmth her brother offered. When she closed her eyes, she could still feel the heat of the flames that danced around the group. It was the beloved Sanctuary that had burned, the spiritual centre of the town of Penny Grove.

The Sanctuary of Inauron was a building so beloved that it was tended to by everyone, believer or otherwise. Their banishment spoke volumes about the loss the town had felt, and the pain and grief they all experienced. Despite the fire being caused by one of them, they all felt the shame of the building's loss.

Lawson began to laugh, cutting the silence in the clearing. At first, just an arrhythmic chuckle, then slowly it became a more pronounced laugh.

"Something funny?" Addison asked with an eyebrow raised.

"Yeah, this whole fucking situation is funny," Lawson shot back. He cast his eyes upon his fingers where he rolled a blade of grass up into a ball, then smoothed it flat and did it once more, "Think about it, we're here because one of you lot thought it was a great idea to start a fire in the middle of a building whose singular and defining feature is a big fucking tree."

He let that sit with them before he continued, "And look at the sky; it's sunset... Do you know where we'd be right now if this shit had never happened? In the Sanctuary with the rest of our Inauron-loving families, saying this very same prayer, but here we are, in the middle-of-fuckin' nowhere, and our minds are trained well enough to still sit here and pray."

Corin sat up at this; she was wholly devout and in training, like Dawn, to be a Devotee in the Sanctuary; she couldn't abide hearing Lawson speak this way, "maybe some of us care enough about our morals and spirit not to let the habit lie even amidst this horrible event."

Corin's hand grasped the charm at her neck; it was a small woven circle made from the fledgeling branches of Inauron's tree, a subspecies of oak that sat at the centre of Sanctuaries across the known world; it was tied around her neck by a thin leather strap. Corin's hair was held neatly back with a small leather ribbon that ran along her scalp just above her fringe and then wove, along with her hair into a plait at the back.

"There was something about that prayer this time... something different," Addison said, turning his head towards Lawson, unable to hide the ire in his voice. "I'm one of the least spiritual here, but that doesn't mean I'm treating it with contempt, I'm still willing to sit here and pray out of respect for everyone else and my family."

"You mean the family who abandoned you?" Bronson asked without moving his head from his pack next to his sister. Bronson's shorn head was scarred in places as befitting a lumberer; minor nicks and injuries were commonplace, and he was wet with sweat across its surface. "None of us were saved by our parents. They cut all ties with us as soon as they learned one of our group was responsible for the fire. I didn't even see our parents shed a tear; in fact, I'm pretty sure that I saw the hurt in my mother's eyes, but not hurt for the loss of her beloved twins, her only children, but hurt for the loss of her Sanctuary."

Now Wendy joined the conversation, "And whilst we're on the topic, who did start the fire? It had to be one of us, and it certainly wasn't me." Wendy lifted both eyebrows in anger.

"Yeah, whose bright fucking idea was that?" Lawson chided.

"Maybe it was an accident," Addison said, "maybe whoever did it feels guilty, and that's why they're not saying."

"Sounds like something a fire-starter would say," Lawson goaded him.

"My conscience is clear," he retorted. "Maybe all this bluster you're giving us Law, is because you did it?"

Lawson chuckled once more and lay back down onto his pack in the grass.

"Think what you want," he said.

Corin was next to speak, "I've devoted my entire life to the Sanctuary, and the teachings of Inauron, and one of you, my so-called friends, cared nothing for destroying everything I worked towards."

"Fuck this, I'm going for a piss," Stokely said, his childlike demeanour hidden beneath his annoyance at this conversation. He rose and disappeared beyond the tree line. Shortly after, Lawson rose to join him.

Fleta listened to the group, attempting to eliminate people from her suspicions surreptitiously. It didn't take long for the bickering to continue.

"What about those we've not yet heard from?" Corin continued. "Kenley?"

Kenley lowered his gaze, a shy boy unwilling to step out from under Addison's wing. He shook his dark, tightly curled, almost wool-like hair, but didn't meet Corin's gaze. Kenley's main feature was his bright white smile that stood out from his soft brown skin, but this wasn't the face he showed them this evening. Fleta didn't suspect his guilt, she was sure he was close-by at the time of the fire, but she feared for Corin's accusations and how they would affect him.

"He was with Dawn and I the entire time," Addison said, stepping in to defend him.

"I didn't see the fire start; I only heard shouting when it caught onto the tapestries on the walls," Kenley said. Fleta felt his testimony was honest, and she was glad of that. Ever since Dawn and Addison had joined as a couple and merged their friend groups, she'd grown to like Kenley; he was kind, and he was one of the few in the group who could see through her damaged exterior to the heart that lay within.

"Piper?" Corin diverted her attention, sated by his explanation.

"Don't you fucking dare talk to her," Wendy said, placing an arm around her sister. Piper was quiet, sullen, and just as upset as the rest of the group. As Fleta thought back, she had no recollection of Piper ever interacting with them. Wendy did all the talking for the pair of them and did everything in her power to coddle her.

They weren't sisters in the traditional sense; as Fleta understood it, Piper's parents passed away when she was just a baby, and Wendy's parents took her in. Wendy being a year older became instantly protective over her new adoptive sister. Wendy often reluctantly had to explain to others the intricacies of their family dynamic since Piper looked so different to her. Wendy had straightened dark hair and flawless dark skin; she carried herself with an air of grace, given that her father was the Alderman of Penny Grove. They were the wealthiest family in a sea of deprivation - likely not wealthy at all outside the bounds of their small town, but within, they were as royalty. Piper by contrast, was small, worn and unassuming; her long dark hair was the only thing she had in common with Wendy. Piper didn't talk - taking the idea of 'shyness' to a whole new level, Wendy took it upon herself to be her sister's mouthpiece.

Fleta didn't see how either could have set the fire on purpose, but maybe, as Addison had suggested, it could have been an accident.

Wendy's chastisement cowed Corin, and she looked shamefully to the ground.

"Convenient that Lawson and Stokely have left suddenly, don't you think?" Corin said quietly.

"I don't have the energy for this discussion," Addison said after a long sigh, "We've been walking for nearly an entire day, and if Councillor Adair's instructions are to be trusted, we've got another day's walk at least before we reach the lake at the centre of this Inauron-forsaken forest. We'll have plenty of time to fight about whose fault this is tomorrow, the day after, and the day after that too. So let's get some sleep before we tear each other apart."

That was something they could all get on board with. Fleta rolled over onto the pack she shared with her brother as a pillow to try and make herself comfortable against the lumpy earth. She snuggled back and forth, trying to find a comfortable nook in the grass.

She barely noticed Lawson and Stokely return sharing furtive glances as she allowed the exhaustion to wash over her, and finally the sleep began to take her away.

As her eyes closed and she lowered her guard, memories of the fire were replaced by the memories of her encounter just before their exile. She felt the hot blood against the warm iron bludgeon, could smell the gore's oddly metallic scent that sickened her to her stomach, the tackiness of the blood against her skin as she tried to wipe it away with bloody fingers, the coolness of the night's air as she stripped herself bare, before changing into fresh garments, to rid herself of the viscera.

Like others in their makeshift camp, she had her own baggage to carry, and she silently prayed to Inauron that hers wouldn't consume her whole.

2

An Unspoken Story

Fleta kept her eyes tightly closed as Javi rose from beside her. She could hear him fumbling with his belt buckle, an almost pleasant metallic jingle of tones that were wholly unfitting to the event that had just occurred between them. He turned to her; she lay on her back in the bed, eyes red from tears.

"You know the drill. If you tell anyone about this," Javi said intensely, quietly, "I'll kill your brother."

She waited until the door of her bedroom closed behind him before she burst into tears.

The first time it happened, she'd been left confused. She was too young to understand what was happening to her; she only knew that it made her feel unclean. As the years marched on, she learned that resistance makes things worse for her in the long run. Whenever she saw Javi, she retreated into her shell, her natural wilfulness torn from her. She had cruelly learned that it was better to lie there and take herself away to another place, close her eyes and dream of a different life.

She pictured trees higher than she could see, fields of roses, beach-side sunsets, and mountain precipices that gave way to beautiful vistas and sprawling valleys. Each imaginary place became her little retreat, her paradise to where she could escape the abuse. Without her vivid imagination, she didn't believe she'd have the ability to survive what she was going through so frequently.

Usually, his smell snapped her out of her dreams, the sickly-stale scent of ale from Bark's Tavern, along with the fetid, earthy aroma of gravel, his self-destructive vice. He was her uncle, her father's brother, he should care for her, but he was tormenting her with his every breath. Her all-but absent parents made him more brazen in his abuse. He'd send Bronson on errands leaving the two of them alone, and by the time he returned, she would have forced herself to wipe away the tears and pretend as if nothing had happened. She did everything she possibly could to keep this away from her brother.

The dense forest of the Wildlands almost

surrounded Penny Grove, and the many lumber camps around the town's perimeter provided the lion's share of the town's meagre wealth. Carpenters, shipbuilders and artisans all across Gilgannon sought the highly regarded Grove wood; however, because of the town's location many miles south of any other settlement, it was a complex trade to make, with too little a margin for most trade caravans. It was an industry that barely kept the townspeople fed and clothed, but it was the only viable industry they had.

When her parents, Wentworth and Gracie, had moved to Penny Grove from Wenda's Rook, they had taken on the surname Timber as an homage to their plan to become embroiled with Penny Grove wood industry - everything they had known about the Grove was rumour and here-say. They had grand plans for taking over the lumber trade of the town with Wentworth's experience of hard labour and Gracie's business acumen. However, they didn't anticipate the competition and ambition from the Caviliers, Dawn's family, who already held much of a monopoly over Grove wood. As a result, the Timber family could carve out only a tiny share of the market, barely enough to earn a living. It was a risky move, and it became a huge burden for their parents to salvage their aspirations.

To focus their efforts on their struggling business, Wentworth sent a missive to his brother, Javi, to help wherever they needed it. Javi had arrived when Fleta was eight years old, and he took up much of the childcare duties, freeing Wentworth and Gracie to knuckle down and provide for the family. At Fleta and Bronson's age, his duties comprised only feeding them and just making sure they stayed alive. Of course, neither parent had expected what Javi would do to their precious daughter. Fleta often fantasised about telling her fiercely protective father and watching him take revenge on her behalf. What kept her from that fate was Javi's dark and unpredictable personality; she worried that a fight between her father and uncle would cause her father's death... and so silent she would remain.

Javi was never gentle, but if he hurt her, it was always in places covered by her clothes; her ribs, thighs, and back. These were not the actions of a man fuelled by and overtaken with his ugly passions; this was a deliberate destruction of her entire being. It wasn't opportunistic; it felt especially cold and personal, breaking her into pieces he could easily handle as he pleased. The abuse started almost immediately, and Fleta had never figured out what she did to him that made him treat her this way; she was but a child - why her?

Further evidence of this was the vastly different opinion people around her had of him,

Javi was loved throughout the town; he was charismatic, personable and could always spare time for those in need. Even her dear twin Bronson loved Javi, he looked up to him, but Fleta wished he could see even a hint of what his idol put her through. As time wore on, Javi and Bronson became closer still. Her previously unbreakable bond with her brother was severed gradually over the course of nearly a decade. How could she rely on her twin, if her twin idolised her abuser? It wasn't Bronson's fault, of course, he was little more than a child himself and Javi was a master manipulator, but that didn't make their uncle and nephew kinship any less bitter for Fleta to witness.

The dual nature of his personality became apparent to Fleta almost immediately; he could project this fun-loving, kind, jokey persona outwards, deftly disguising the poison in his heart with expert efficiency. Fleta felt she was the only one that truly knew Javi, and that fact alone made her sick to her stomach; it bespoke a closeness to him she never wanted.

Her illusory retreats, fields of long grass swaying in the breeze, daisies on a warm spring morning, and anything else she could conjure became her surrogate home, the only place she felt truly secure.

The comfort of her mother's embrace, Bronson's warmth and her father's inner strength became more distant from her as time went on, partly because of her guilt at holding her trauma back, but also because of her fear that being too close is liable to put them at risk from Javi's wrath. They could feel her separation from them and often brought it up. Her family were at a loss to her complete and utter withdrawal from the confident, funny and kind personality they'd known so well in the years leading up to Javi's arrival. Her uncle had her trapped; if she told anyone, she risked their lives, and if she didn't tell anyone, Javi could continue his abuse... whichever way she looked at it, she lost, and Javi won.

She didn't know where she stood now that they were exiled though. She was no longer in danger from Javi, nor was Bronson, but how can she even explain the years of abuse and isolation in a way that'll make Bronson understand? Her fear that kept her silent even now, was that Bronson would choose not to believe her.

❋ ❋ ❋

As Fleta awoke from a night of self-induced torment, she rolled over to check on Bronson. She would do what anyone else would do in her state; she threw herself into her task, to mask the pain. She could think of doing naught but caring for her ailing brother as he forced his way through his gravel withdrawal sickness, an addiction that Javi had coerced him into. She dabbed at his forehead with a damp cloth, trying vainly to keep him cool.

"Anyone seen Corin?" Dawn asked not long after they awoke.

The exiles were a sea of shrugs.

"She's not here," she continued, "and she's not the type to leave without saying anything."

"Maybe she got tired of accusing us of being firestarters," Stokely quipped.

Dawn scowled at him.

"She's probably gone on to the lake," Addison said. "We all knew that's where we were headed. Our arguments last night probably made her feel as if she'd prefer her own company."

Fleta watched on, with only half her attention as she stroked her fingertips around

Bronson's cheek and chin in a comforting manner. The group continued to bicker around her, and her eyes rolled at each backhanded swipe and each thinly veiled showing of animosity. If this was to be the eternal dynamic of the group, Fleta wanted nothing to do with it, she could certainly see how Corin would want to leave.

She closed her eyes and tried to drown out the arguments, but when she re-opened them, she could see the others preparing their bags and clothing to move on. Addison wore his rucksack, and held his makeshift walking stick, Wendy was packing her water skin into her bag.

She had to stop them, there's no way Bronson could leave in the state he was in. He was barely holding it together, still in and out of consciousness, mumbling to himself and sweating as his fever pressed on.

"We're not leaving yet," Fleta said, assertively.

The group stopped in their tracks and turned their attention towards her.

"Bronson's unwell," she said matter-of-factly. It wasn't something they could argue over because no matter how convincing they were, Bronson still wouldn't miraculously recover and be well enough to hike to the centre of the Wildlands.

Dawn cocked her head to the side in concern,

"what's wrong with him, Flea?"

She shrugged, then lied, "he gets like this sometimes; it usually only lasts a day or so."

She had far too much on her mind to consider anything other than her brother's safety; her head was abuzz with regrets, shame, and pain. She felt emotionally disconnected from the debate arising within the camp, barely hearing the complaints, Addison's attempt to convince her, or any of the other admonishments from her companions. All the while she was doing her best to bury her rising emotions, her panic, her swirling thoughts. Despite her best efforts, she became increasingly anxious with every further word from them. Her breathing quickened, her extremities chilled, and she could hear her heart thumping in her chest. She diverted her nervous energy into dabbing a cool cloth at Bronson's burning forehead, a poor attempt at masking the anxiety.

"He's probably faking it," Stokely said. "Probably wants a day to put his feet up after burning down the Sanctuary."

She snapped.

She recalled little the ensuing argument; she was overcome with emotion in a way she hadn't been for years. It was like the floodgates had opened, releasing all the pent up and stored away emotion from behind the dam of her childhood pain. Maybe this newfound assertiveness had been there all along, systematically buried by her abuser Javi, and now with all the risks he placed upon her gone, it crept back to the surface. At least she hoped so, because the other alternative was that she was broken, and that this anger was just a symptom of her impending breakdown.

Whichever it was, the argument ended with the camp being split. Lawson, Wendy, Piper and Stokely went off to follow Corin to the lake. Whereas Addison, Dawn, and Kenley remained with her and her brother. They'd split in two.

She felt responsible for the camp's division and spent the ensuing hours running over the argument in her mind, trying to find out if she could have managed it better, but there were gaps in her recollection that were difficult to reconcile. She couldn't remember what she'd said or to whom she said it, she could barely remember their replies. It was like a whirlwind of emotion, and now she was left numb in the resultant calm. Again, she disconnected herself from the camp, focusing her attention back on her brother.

If Bronson had been well, he would have scoffed at her care for him, she'd been such a terrible sister, so separate from her family over these last years. Perhaps that's why she spent so much time on his recovery, perhaps this was her penance for the time she'd wasted beneath the yoke of her abuser.

Time itself had a strange place within her mind, looking back she could barely recall what others would regard as important life steps, like when she and Bronson turned sixteen they'd had a large party in the Sanctuary with all her friends present; but all she remembered was the panic setting in before they entered the building. Bronson had gone in without her, and she'd followed a few minutes after, once the birthday wishes for her brother had subsided. She remembered the pain, but never the happiness, as if her mind had a selective filter that was designed to keep her miserable and ashamed. Time felt as though it was slipping away from her, even here at her brother's side, she seemed to disassociate with the goings on around her, hours falling away never to be seen again.

3

Schism

Bronson's sleep was disturbed that first night in the Wildlands. The group of nine others around him that night had all collapsed on their packs and seemingly slept easily, but not Bronson. He felt too warm or cold, or the ground wasn't comfortable enough. His shoulder ached from being pressed against the dirt, preventing him from reaching the peace of sleep. He sat up and looked at the others. Light snores emanated from the group, but his sister watched him.

Fleta liked to brag that she was born mere minutes before Bronson; his usual retort was that she left the oven a few minutes early, but he was cooked to perfection. They always seemed to know what the other was thinking. Bronson once caught himself on a falling tree at their family's lumber camp, its flailing branches clawing at his arm on its way to the ground. Upon returning home, he found his sister had been suddenly overcome with worry for him all day without realising why. This preternatural twin-sense had always mystified them, but they'd simply accepted it as part of their lives together.

His mind span, and not even his sister's cool hand placed across his forehead stabilised him. He inspected her, her brow had wrinkled, and she wore concern all across her face.

Fleta gently unbuttoned his filthy, worn, white shirt at the neck, giving his chest space to feel the grace of the cold night air. As the air rushed onto his clammy skin, he inhaled, feeling his body cool, albeit temporarily.

"It's starting then..." she murmured, quietly enough not to disturb the others sleeping so close by.

"I thought I'd have a few days," Bronson responded, his voice shaking from the shivers.

A chill ran down his spine, and he could not prevent his body from reacting almost comically, flexing his shoulders and tightening his arms about his torso. In the scant light afforded by the moonlight, all Bronson could see was the painful concern from his quiet, meek, often uncaring sister. He wasn't sure whether her concern for him was because of how sick he looked, or if she was simply trying to distract herself from the trauma of their banishment. Either way, his withdrawal had approached far faster than either had expected.

"Can't be helped... Here, lie down." She made space on the pack they used as a pillow and then crawled over it to lie alongside him. She nestled into the crook of his arm, placing her head on his shoulder and her arm across his chest. This was the closest Bronson and Fleta had been for years. Ever since their individual problems began, they'd disregarded each other's desire for familial affection. It felt nice, it had a calming effect on him.

His eyes blinked slowly as the exhaustion of the last few days washed over him. A sensation overcame him, giving his body an excessive weight but his head an unnerving weightlessness. He noticed his involuntary nods as if his body was fighting with the muscles in his neck, trying to keep his head from floating off into the sky. It was disorientating. Fleta held him closer, which comforted him, but not enough to allow him to drift off to sleep. He had to stay awake to keep his head on his shoulders...

He looked over and spied his uncle, Javi, watching him from between the trees. The interloper smirked and winked at him before disappearing between blinks.

"Javi?" He said aloud.

Fleta lifted herself to look into his eyes.

"Javi's not here; it's just us, Bron," she said quietly.

"He was there..." Bronson started, but the conviction to continue his argument died mid-sentence. "Sorry."

The time between his blinks grew longer and longer, as did the time his eyes remained closed at each blink; he was edging closer to sleep whether or not he wanted to admit it to himself.

As his eyes finally fell closed, they shot back open again, but this time, the sun blazed above him, and Fleta was no longer in the crook of his arm. Everyone in the camp was awake and locked in a fierce argument; the sun shone through the trees, casting rays across his eyes. He struggled to see in the blinding light, but he could make out only pieces of the altercation that was taking place.

"Look at him!" Fleta angrily gestured to Bronson, who felt the group's eyes upon him keenly, causing him to recoil.

"Yeah, he doesn't look well," Dawn replied. Her eyes met Bronson's, and the concern in her expression darkened his mood - if Dawn could tear her attention away from Addison - he must look genuinely dreadful.

"He's not well. In fact, he's quite ill; we should stay here in this clearing for a couple of days.

Let's make sure we're all well enough to get moving."

"Councillor Adair told us to follow the river and head for the lake at the centre of the Wildlands - she seemed certain we'd be safe there." Addison said calmly but with no conviction behind his voice. "What if she's arranged something, and we're not there to see it?"

"I understand that," Fleta argued, red-faced, "but how the hell will my brother get out there? Some paths we walked yesterday were treacherous, and he can barely keep his head upright."

Addison didn't have an answer; he looked at Bronson, who stared back, glassy-eyed, still disorientated from his seemingly momentary lapse of consciousness.

"Are you just going to leave him?" Fleta pressed him.

Addison paused. He glanced toward the sky, eyebrows raised, then adjusted his jaw.

"I don't know," he barked suddenly, causing more than a few heads around the camp to perk up to the commotion. "Everyone's looking at me like I'm the decision-maker here. I don't know what I'm doing. I don't know where I'm going. I don't know why I'm here!"

"You're the oldest," Dawn said in a tone that

bespoke the answer's obviousness.

"What the fuck has that got to do with anything?" he yelled, before regaining some measure of composure. "Lawson is only a few weeks younger than me."

"Hey, don't pull me into this," Lawson said as he stepped into the clearing from beyond the treeline. Lawson had an uneasiness about him that was wholly out of character for him. Perhaps he too was feeling the effects of the banishment, unable to mask it with his usual blend of charisma and vitriol. Almost everyone in the camp took a great interest in how this conflict unfolded - would they all stay, leave, or split?

"Everyone can just do what they want." Addison threw his arms up. "If you want to stay, then stay! If you want to go, then go! I'm not the group's father; I couldn't give a shit."

"We all know that's not true," Dawn said, trying to comfort him. She looked towards Fleta, "perhaps we'll stay a couple of days and see if Bronson recovers."

Addison turned and walked away, clearly needing the space. Bronson had a cold impression of Addison. He'd never liked him, not since they were young, and it took getting older before he realised why; Addison had stolen Dawn's heart away from him.

Fleta was suddenly at his side - he didn't see her move toward him, she was in the centre of the camp one moment, and at the next, she was kneeling at his side, dabbing his forehead with a cloth. The sun had moved to its apex - he must have fallen out of consciousness again.

The camp was almost empty; the others had left, just Fleta remained; he hoped they'd just gone to get firewood or to find some water, but his anxiety was rising - worsened by the fever. He worried deeply that his condition had split the group.

He batted her hand away and stumbled onto his front, then up to his feet, his knees shaking, his centre of mass unstable, swaying to and fro. He pushed his way to the trees, shoving Dawn out of the way as he did so before falling to his knees and projecting his vomit into the bushes.

Fleta was at his side again.

"It's okay; I know you can get through this. I'm going to be here the whole time..."

4

Setting Up

"He's gone." Dawn said, falling to her knees next to her.

Fleta snapped herself out of her stupor, and her heart leapt at the idea that her twin had passed, right in front of her very eyes. She almost pulled a neck muscle shooting her gaze to her brother's sweaty visage. He squirmed in and out of consciousness, but he was certainly alive.

"Wh...what?" she said, turning to look back at Dawn with a frown.

"Addison. My Addy. He's gone," Dawn replied, before tears took her into Fleta's reluctant embrace.

"What do you mean, gone?"

"It's my fault; I think this is it for us. He left.

I think he went to catch up with Lawson and the others..."

Fleta wasn't sure how she could juggle caring for her brother and comforting her friend. She had too much responsibility and didn't have the mental capacity to hold so much compassion. Still, she tried as hard as she could to at least sound sympathetic.

"What happened, Dawn?"

"We argued." She buried her face into Fleta's breast, crying. Fleta placed an arm around her, feeling Dawn's nose press into her breastbone. "We always argue, it's so stupid. But this time, he said our betrothal was just business between our parents, and now we had no obligation to continue."

She dropped the cloth she was using to dab at her brother's head and placed her other arm around Dawn in a tight embrace.

"And the thing is," she continued between sniffles, "he was right, I think. I think we were only together for our parents sake. Neither of us had ever said it out loud, though. I really loved him, but hearing him say that made me question everything."

Fleta had no words, she could only listen. Her energy felt painfully divided by the maelstrom of emotion sweeping around her.

Dawn and Addison's relationship had been

tumultuous from the off. There was love there, for sure, but there was also a healthy serving of frustration and simple incompatibility. Hearing of a new conflict between them was tantamount to hearing about lunch; it happened so often it was hardly newsworthy. Fleta recalled an argument they'd had not even a week ago; Dawn had told Addison that he needed to prove his love to her by shouting about it in the town square at midday, when the square was busy with trade and travel. Addison just shrugged and ignored the request, clearly disinterested in Dawn's need for overt romantic declarations. Addison asked her what other loving couples she'd ever seen in Penny Grove do something like that, and she told him she didn't want to compare herself to others. Eventually, Addison had relented and complied with the gesture, but by then, the romance of it had faded, leaving both feeling unsatiated by the whole affair. It was an event that perfectly encapsulated their dynamic; Dawn valued gestures, and Addison valued quiet, cosy contentment - neither seemed to want to cater for the other's needs for expressions of romance.

"Did I waste my teenage years with him, if he had no love for me? Did I even truly love him? I'm so confused," Dawn said, rubbing her tears into Fleta's gown.

Fleta felt overwhelmed, but could do nothing but hold her best friend as she cried. In the back of her mind, a worry surfaced - if she was the only one holding the three of them together, then what would happen when Fleta's mind finally broke down? If Addison had left, then who would lead? Who would pick up the pieces of Fleta's scattered consciousness? On this worry, time slipped again and had no way of knowing how long Dawn had been in her arms.

Coming to, she looked over Dawn's shoulder and saw Kenley busying himself making the clearing into some sort of campsite for them. She hadn't noticed him before; she had assumed that he'd left with Addison, his closest friend. Instead, here he was, in the background, setting things up for their comfort. He'd dragged logs from beyond the treeline to serve as seating, built a fire, and was preparing a pile of sticks to keep close-by. She smiled. He was helping. He was the only one that was helping.

Kenley may well be unaware of the impact of what he was doing, but she knew that if they were going to stay in this clearing until Bronson recovered, they'd need some essentials like warmth and light. Whilst she held Dawn and managed Bronson's fever, she was glad that someone else in the camp had taken responsibility for all the rest.

Before she knew it, they were sat around the fire on the logs, with Bronson laying nearby, she had an arm around Dawn who was still reeling from her breakup, Kenley fed the fire and the light above them had dimmed. Her distance from what was happening seemed to shorten, and she felt more comfort and presence with herself than she'd done since the Sanctuary of Inauron had burned. She had been in a near constant daze since the inferno, and it was only now, more than a day later, that her mind began to feel more hers. The three of them sat silently around the dancing flames, as a quiet contentment fell over them.

"Thank you," Fleta said to Kenley, who looked up, confused. "For setting up the fire."

"Oh," he said, smiling. "Well, somebody had to."

"You didn't leave with Addison?"

At mention of his name, Dawn buried her face into Fleta's shoulder even further.

"He left without telling from what I understand; just up and disappeared," Kenley said, looking pained.

"Would you have left if he'd spoken to you?" she asked.

"Not sure," Kenley said. "I think I would have convinced him to stay."

"Why?"

Kenley gestured to Bronson. Then, pressed his lips together in a show of sympathy as he returned his gaze back to Fleta. He ran his fingers through his curly dark hair, pulling it out of his face, "how's he doing?"

"He's in an out of consciousness," she said. Then, to divert any attention away from the illness' cause, "it's something he does from time to time. He'll be okay."

She snuggled into her brother's arms when the light in the sky finally died, and the exhaustion from the day overcame her. The day before they'd walked for almost the entire time the light allowed, but today she'd barely moved. Despite this, she felt far more drained this night, the day before was physically draining, but today was emotionally draining. She felt like she could barely keep her eyes open as she settled into her brother's warmth; she hadn't held him like this for years. She needed this comfort as she sunk into a deep slumber.

"Fleta," the voice cried sharply.

Opening her eyes, the morning sun cast a ray onto the figure atop her producing a misty silhouette. It was Javi, she could smell the Bark's ale that seemed to leak out of his every pore. She lashed out instinctively, hitting him with all her might, using her fingernails to scratch at his face; she could almost smell the blood she drew from him.

"What the fuck," the voice cried again.

"Fleta, stop," a female voice this time. "Snap

out of it!"

She stopped and felt Dawn's strong embrace as she came to her senses. Kenley lay on the ground before her, face scratched with blood on his hands and neck from the wound.

"What the fuck," Kenley said again.

As the realisation of what just happened washed over her, she began to tear up, and her bottom lip shook.

"I'm sorry, Kenley, I don't know what happened," he just stared at her in disbelief and pressed his hand against his face where she'd scratched him. She looked around, "where's Bron?"

"That's what I was trying to ask you," Kenley said quietly, still taken aback.

Dawn separated from their embrace to look directly into Fleta's glassy eyes, "he's gone."

5

A Fever Dream

"I have something to tell you both," Dawn had announced all those years ago. It was the height of summer four years past. Fleta and Bronson moved closer to hear what she had to say; at their young age of thirteen, Fleta, Bronson and Dawn all played together any moment they were able. They all stood behind The Sanctuary of Inauron in the centre of Penny Grove. The mud from their play streaked up their legs; Bronson was the dirtiest, but they'd all be playing around where they shouldn't.

She bit her bottom lip in anticipation.

"Well, what is it?" Fleta asked.

Dawn beamed. "I'm getting married!"

"What?" Fleta gasped.

Bronson remained silent; he had no air in his lungs to form words, Dawn had just taken it from him.

"To who?" Fleta said. "Come on, tell me everything!"

"Addison."

Bronson composed himself, then sneered. "Addison, that tall ginger kid who's always hanging about at your father's place?"

"Yes." Dawn shouted, unable to contain her smile, stretching it so wide the tendons around her throat protruded. Fleta squealed and threw her arms around Dawn.

"How the hell did that happen?" Bronson asked.

"Well, you know my father works with Emil Ruthand, who does all the sales and numbers and what-not for my dad?"

"Yeah, I know who he is," Bronson replied.

"Well, Addison is Emil's son. He and my father had this incredible idea to join us as a family so that we could grow our lumber trade."

"Oh, so it's just a business marriage?" He emphasised the word 'just', hoping she'd catch it.

"Not really. I mean, yes, it is, but I like Addison, and I'm pretty sure he likes me too. It's business, sure, family, but that doesn't mean it has to be loveless." Dawn frowned, carefully weighing up Bronson's response. She wasn't unaware of Bronson's feelings for her, feelings that they'd both been close to acting upon in recent years.

"You're only thirteen," Bronson said. "Isn't it a bit early for a betrothal?"

"Well, Addison is only a year or so older, and he doesn't have a problem with it. We're not getting married yet; it'll be a few years away. That's a betrothal; it's like a promise to get married when we're old enough."

Bronson didn't say anymore. He couldn't. If he allowed himself one more word on the matter, he was liable to damage his relationship with Dawn forever. As far as Bronson was concerned, he and Addison would now be enemies for life. He felt the heavy stone of the Sanctuary wall against his back as he leaned, willing the structure to keep him upright.

"We can all still hang out; nothing will change."

It did.

It all changed.

First, Addison and Dawn came together, awkwardly joining the group of them, then slowly Dawn began to pull away, hanging off Addison's every word and all but ignoring Bronson. As he wallowed in his self-pity, his uncle had given him the opportunity to experience gravel for the very first time.

It was this gravel that caused his downfall.

Four years after Dawn's announcement, he was undesirable, with darkened eyes, cracked lips, and a spindly, hunched gait resulting from his addiction. Dawn, by cruel contrast, had matured into a beautiful, petite, dark-haired young woman with a diminutive frame that didn't match her fiery spirit - he loved that about her. She behaved with an inner fire, a strength, that was wholly unfitting with her stature. She had cut her hair short, which accentuated her beautiful features. Many of the more fervent followers of Inauron wore short hair; where others had purposefully styled it this way to reduce the amount of interest from sexual partners; for Dawn, coupled with her pronounced cheekbones and beautiful dark eyes, it only made her more alluring.

Whenever he spared a thought for her, upon her pedestal, it pulled him deeper into the darkness that plagued him. He felt unworthy of her, so why couldn't he lay his feelings to rest? She was a queen to him, but he considered himself just a lowly serf.

Bronson vividly remembered the night his uncle, Javi, introduced him to gravel. He was young and freshly embittered by the news of Dawn's engagement; left seemingly with no companionship or ability to vent his pain.

Their family constantly struggled to keep their heads above water; his parents spent almost every minute of the day at the lumber camp on the outskirts of town. Wentworth was a saw-miller, whilst Gracie organised the accounts for the lumber projects; they were a well-oiled team. The lumber camp always had far more wood coming in than capacity in the mill to cut it all down. The long hours and sometimes terrifying working conditions meant that Bronson's parents were all but absent. Bronson knew they did what they could, but unable to contain his pain over losing his prospects with Dawn, he needed his family.

On top of his parents being absent, he had been a painful witness to his sister Fleta pulling away from him the last few years. She was his twin; they were supposed to be joined at the hip, but he'd seen her ability to be present with him slowly slip away until she could barely even look at him. He long suspected she was hiding something from him. He struggled to remember the last time he'd seen her smile or seen her happy - she'd put on quite a show when Dawn had announced her engagement, but he could read her well enough to know when it was artificial. She would shut down any time he ever tried to bridge their widening gap.

With Dawn's betrothal, he'd lost the person he had assumed he'd spend the rest of his life with. His parents were always at work or too tired after long days at the mill, and his devoted sister seemed to hate being near him; he had never felt so lonely. All he had was Uncle Javi.

Javi was not a good surrogate parent; he was a good friend, but not a good parent. Nothing was comforting about him. He was all about jokes and fun, but when it came to anything serious, it often seemed like he didn't have the capacity for warmth. Still, he was all Bronson had.

The traditional houses of the centre of Penny Grove were two-story lime-coated, thatched roofed buildings that were densely packed around The Sanctuary. However, their home, whilst looking the same as others, was subdivided vertically into three different properties. Each had its door and a small window, creating a three-house terrace out of a cottage of which they occupied the middle. It bore the scars of the hasty conversion to a terrace; a staircase precariously affixed to the upper landing, a kitchen/dining/living area that seemed too small to hold what they needed, and two upstairs bedrooms of odd shapes. Bronson and Fleta's room was an L shape, with nary enough space for the two beds they required, and right now, the way Fleta acted around him, he no longer felt comfortable spending time there; it made their already paltry living space seem all the smaller for it.

He sat on a long wooden bench near the door to the street. Bronson's father had made the bench and table set from the unsalable offcuts and scrap from their lumber camp. It wasn't made for comfort.

"What's the matter, bud?" Javi asked him, concern in his eyes as he pulled up a small stool and sat beside him. The earthy aroma that accompanied Javi was almost overpowering; he moved his tongue inside his mouth to clear the scent before swallowing whatever he'd just ingested.

Javi lived with them, but he slept downstairs near the back of the house, on a roughly-fashioned cot covered with cheap fabrics. Since Bronson and Fleta came of age, Javi was no longer needed as their caretaker, but that unfortunately didn't make him feel he should contribute to their living arrangement. He occasionally helped Wentworth and Gracie at the camp but spent the other days either at Bark's Tavern or lying around the house not even pretending to be helpful. Bronson did most of the errands, Javi telling him to go here and go there whilst he didn't move a muscle himself.

Bronson wasn't sure he could answer him; if he did, he wasn't sure Javi would take his concerns seriously; his pain, after all, came from his feeling of isolation from everything he knew and held dear. As experience had dictated, if Javi couldn't fix it, he'd probably make a big joke, so Bronson quickly had to think of a reason to deflect.

"It's Fleta; I'm worried about her; she doesn't seem to want to spend time with me," he said, knowing Fleta was but a small part of the problems he was battling. He ran his hands over his shorn head, elbows resting on his knees. "Twins are supposed to be able to talk to each other."

"I know what you mean," Javi said, "I think you need to know something about women. Growing up, they undergo all sorts of crazy changes - men do too, but theirs are more... emotional."

"Yeah, I get that."

"Perhaps without your mother around to be sympathetic to her 'womanly struggles', she has no choice but to live with them alone."

Bronson considered this; young though he was, he could certainly believe that these 'womanly struggles' that Javi talked about might have had this effect on her.

"Do you want me to talk to her?" Javi asked.

Bronson smirked, thinking Javi was joking, which he replaced immediately with a furrowed brow when he realised he was not.

"If she doesn't open up to me, her twin, who

shared a womb with her, then she probably won't open up to you," he scoffed.

"That may be *precisely* the reason she will open up to me," Javi rose confidently, swallowing once more and wiping his mouth and nose with his shirtsleeve. The rickety wooden stairs to their small dwelling's upper floor creaked awkwardly with every step. Bronson listened for a conversation through the boards but heard only deep murmurs.

After around five minutes of waiting, the steps creaked again, and Javi came into view.

"No luck, bud," he confirmed precisely what Bronson had expected, but now his brow was more furrowed and his teeth clenched. He wondered what she had said to him to make him react this way; he seemed angry.

Bronson saw him take a second to compose himself before he cheered back up, looking as if nothing had changed.

"Hey, y'know what," he said, gesturing to the side with his head in a vague request for Bronson to follow him, "let me show you something."

Javi walked around to where he slept, in a nook beneath their staircase. His personal space was unkempt, bedsheets unmade, and odd grey-like stains across his fabrics, which Bronson supposed were from moisture ingress into their house. Javi bent to retrieve a small wooden box beneath his bed. A poorly made hinge barely supporting the lid's weight squeaked as it opened. Bronson was hit by the strong earthy aroma that Javi brought with him not five minutes earlier.

"Mind the smell," Javi smirked.

Inside was some white scrap fabric acting as a liner, wrapped within was a collection of small stones; or were they crystals? Javi reached in and retrieved one mid-sized stone, handing it to Bronson.

"Tastes better than it smells," he said, gesturing for him to eat.

"You want me to eat a stone?" Bronson retorted.

"Appearances can be deceiving," Javi laughed. "I've already had one, so I shouldn't have another for a few hours, but if it'll help…."

He reached in and took one of the smaller stones, placing it between his teeth, showing that he was eating it, before closing his lips and chewing.

Bronson copied him. The stone appeared to melt when it touched his tongue, turning into a thick paste that seemed to coat the inside of his mouth.

"Tastes a bit weird."

"Give it fifteen or twenty minutes, and you won't even remember the taste."

At its core, gravel was a hallucinogen; the mushrooms that represented its primary ingredient were a known low-potency high that grew naturally in the shade of the trees surrounding Penny Grove. There was little benefit to eating them, but as kids, they all liked to pick them and throw them to the birds. It was a rebellious teenage pastime in the region to watch the magpies and crows fly into things when they couldn't control their soaring speeds.

The hallucinogenic component of these mushrooms was enhanced by the chemicals within the post-fermented mash that the local brewers often discarded. This, combined with a process that purified it, brought this unassuming mushroom's potency into the type of high that the people in the seedy underbelly of nearby towns like Orenide Hills would pay a lot of money for.

And so, after so many months of feeling downtrodden, Bronson finally felt bliss.

The problem with long-term addiction is that if you run out of the drug, withdrawal kicks in at some point...

* * *

He awoke with a start. He looked about with eyes that slowly became accustomed to the low light of the Wildlands; a freshly rising sun, not yet cresting the horizon, lit the sky with a glow that was all but obscured by the density of the vegetation. Fleta was at his side, sleeping softly, his sentry guardian; her light snores comforted him. It felt as though it were a mere moment since the midday light was cast across his face, and he struggled to nod off, though the dryness of his mouth and throat told him otherwise. The clearing had all sorts of fixtures it didn't have before, a fire pit, and fallen logs hauled in from beyond the tree line as make-shift seating. It didn't bear the signs of a new and temporary camp; he surmised that the group had been in this spot for a while - just how much time had he lost?

He surveyed the surrounding camp, dismayed that only four remained from a party of ten. Dawn had accompanied him and his sister, and another figure he couldn't quite make out tossed and turned in the shade; it must be Addison since he and Dawn were inseparable. However, when the figure repositioned for comfort, he saw Kenley.

Curious.

Before he could think on it more, his stomach lurched and churned, begging to be let out. He rolled in the cold grass onto his front. He pushed himself onto his knees, feeling the coldness of the damp mud as it made its way through the fabric of his trousers. He elevated himself onto his hands, head hanging low, and closed his eyes to help him focus on breathing deeply, avoiding the incoming nausea. He opened his mouth and felt a lump pushing its way up his gullet, triggering his gag reflex, but nothing was forthcoming.

Whilst doubled over, he considered the group and how the whole thing had come about because of his withdrawal from gravel. He knew his addiction was to blame for whatever had happened in his lost hours or days to make the group split. He couldn't make amends unless he came out of this withdrawal with his mind and relationships intact. That gave him the determination to push on and improve himself.

He made his way up to his feet, one foot at a time, slowly breathing. The dizziness became apparent when his knees lifted his head high, causing him to sway. He wiped his sweat-soaked brow and rubbed at his scalp. His head and face were hot; the patches of teenage facial hair adorning his cheeks stuck out at odd angles; he was a sight to behold.

The reflex to hurl once more overtook him, and he let his feet rush for the tree line, not paying even a glance back to the others in the camp as he made for the bushes.

Had he done this once already?

A strange sense of déjà vu washed over him as he leaned against a tree for stability. Again, nothing was forthcoming; it must have been a long time since he had eaten anything.

"Psst... you coming?" Javi asked, a voice just beyond his sight. "You must be thirsty."

The sound of water trickling pricked his ears, and he followed the sounds of his uncle's voice, as he led him into the forest's darkness.

6

Driftwood

"Follow me," Kenley commanded. They fell in line behind him.

Dawn knew that Kenley's father, the town's hunter, had the skills to track people through the woods. Still, she had this niggling feeling in her gut that Kenley's skill was lacking. She watched as he fumbled about, scouring the ground for disturbed earth, broken twigs, anything that could point them in the direction Bronson headed.

"Where are we going?" Fleta asked.

"I'm going to track him; follow closely." The gentle young boy was gone; now, he channelled his military-like father as he walked Dawn and Fleta into the dense trees.

"Okay, see the undisturbed ground over

there," he pointed to a patch of ground nestled between some trees just off the clearing. "It's got some recognisable characteristics - leaves and pine needles are matting the surface, and due to how long this area has been undisturbed, there are probably many layers of this one on top of another."

He walked them over to it, crouched to touch it and pushed away some of the top layers. "See, we have almost the same, but this is darker, saturated and partially rotted; the deeper we go, the more it looks like soil. Every layer has its characteristics."

Dawn was impressed; she had underestimated the unassuming boy. Though that didn't seem enough to appease an impatient Fleta whose brother was still lost, alone, and suffering from a sickness. Kenley caught Fleta's eyes, sensing her anxiety.

"I'm teaching you this because when tracking, there are many false positives, and because we need to find Bronson now, we may have to split up." He stuttered briefly whilst explaining. "I will track him, but I want both of you to know what to look for."

He paused, then with a conviction she'd not seen in him before, he looked to Fleta, "we will find him, I promise you."

Dawn put an arm around her friend, comforting her, feeling Fleta's small frame almost shake with worry. She couldn't calm her friend's nerves; she had not the words. Kenley walked with a directness that bounced him from clue to clue, from small welts in the undergrowth to exposed earth or disturbed foliage. Whilst doing so, he tried as much as he could not to wince in pain at the scratch-mark Fleta had left on his face and neck as it pulsed and throbbed.

Fleta had apologised profusely immediately following her waking, but he had dismissed her apologies; he wouldn't accept them. The moment he had realised it was all a big mistake, he wanted to just forgive and forget about it all.

He pointed once more at the ground; another clue.

"If an animal had disturbed this earth, chances are, only one or two layers would be upturned, but Bronson is a fairly tall lad; if he trudged through this soft ground, we'd see far more than a few flipped leaves."

He stood and looked around, spotting another patch close to the first, "here," he summoned them over.

They stood over some thin twigs, "these are light, thin and easily broken. Look around you; they're everywhere, almost as far as the eye can see," he picked one up, held it in his fist and used his raised thumb to press against its length. The audible snap came after very little pressure was exerted. "I barely touched this, and it snapped completely. Now look at the exposed inner surface of the twig; you can identify those that have only recently snapped against those that snapped seasons ago by how clean and bright the inner wood is."

Speeding his lesson up, "one more thing to look out for," he held out his arm, directing them over to another patch of earth; this one was further from the safety of the clearing, some feet in amongst the old-growth trees. He gestured to a small group of plants and a small group of mushrooms nearby.

"These small plants and mushrooms will be like Inauron's favour if we find them; they're so easily disturbed, brittle and soft that they absorb the events around them. Mushrooms that are broken have usually been broken *by* something, especially if the rest of them on the sprout are still relatively strong."

Dawn had her doubts about much of this advice, and it seemed to be either common sense or too vague to nail down a particular track. She had to admit that Kenley was engaging in his presentation; it made her want to believe everything he said despite her inclination towards negativity.

"Anything could have done that, though; in the couple of days we've been out here, we've seen all sorts of wildlife," she said.

Kenley smiled as if he was expecting the question, "any single, lone clue can be explained in many, many ways, but it becomes more difficult to explain it away when there's lots of evidence grouped together." He beamed as if the lecture was going exactly to plan. Dawn wondered whether Kenley's father had taught him these basics in the same way - he certainly seemed to have adopted his father's demeanour for the talk. "We're looking for many clues, similar clues, and groups of clues to figure out which way he went. Follow me."

As Fleta followed Kenley closely, she pulled herself out of Dawn's embrace. The morning air's chill swept in to replace Fleta's warm body, and she couldn't stop herself from recoiling at the coldness. She wrapped her arms around herself as she filed in behind Fleta and rubbed her upper arms, willing the warmth back into them.

"How are we ever going to find him and not get lost?" Fleta cried.

"Look, we can do this." Kenley said, "My father is one of the best hunters the Grove has ever had, and whilst I don't claim to be able to hold a candle to his ability, I'm certain I know enough and have been taught enough over the years that I can help. We can do this, trust me."

Dawn saw Fleta's expression soften; it was clear she trusted him. Fleta and Kenley were largely unfamiliar with one another, but since

Kenley was one of Addison's closest friends, Dawn had spent a lot of time with him and had been exposed to the trappings of Kenley's innermost thoughts, shared with her betrothed. Dawn knew how Kenley doted after Fleta despite Fleta not even knowing he existed; to Dawn it felt more potent than a childhood crush; it bordered on obsession.

He was a year younger than her, at fifteen years old, and before this unexpected excursion into the wilderness, Fleta's only interactions with Kenley had been indirect or through mutual friends; Dawn struggled to remember a time when Kenley and Fleta had ever talked or spent time together one-on-one.

Dawn and Fleta fell comfortably in line behind him when he started following some clues, moving from one to another. He pointed them out; a spot in the mud resembling a footprint, more upturned earth, broken detritus, and muddy residue transferred onto the low-lying plants. They snaked through the ground, between the trees, and around the dense bushes towards a river.

Water swept around them, depositing silt and pebbles on the ground underfoot. Kenley stopped, Fleta and Dawn fell in behind him.

"We need to double back and find some more tracks."

Dawn interjected, "I thought you were

supposed to be good at this!"

"This is what good looks like," he rebutted, "I said before, there are many false positives; we may have inadvertently crossed paths with an animal or even the weather can also make some things look like clues. On top of this, it's also possible that Bronson came to the water's edge, and then walked back into the forest. You're expecting me to draw a straight line all the way to Bronson, but it doesn't work like that - it's more like a lightning strike, with lots of branched diversions going in all directions."

"What can we do?" Fleta asked, "I think I know what I'm looking for now; should we split up?"

"If you're confident, let's go for it," he encouraged her.

"How will we find each other?"

Dawn had disengaged with the tracking process; she had far too many conflicting emotions, and she could barely concentrate on putting one foot in front of the other. This seemed the perfect opportunity for her to compose herself. "I'll stay here; go find your clues, and meet back here when you know where to go. Then we'll continue down the right path."

Kenley nodded at her, and Fleta squeezed her arm. Fleta, her lifelong friend, could sense the turmoil inside her, but she, in turn, had her own crisis to deal with.

Kenley turned his attention to Fleta, "no more than about half an hour or so. We go, find some clues, group them, and follow them. Once we're sure we're on the right path, meet back here."

Pausing, he looked into her eyes.

"Are you sure about this, Fleta; if you want, you can stay with Dawn, and I'll find his trail."

"Let me help," she said, "if I don't do something, I'll go insane."

Dawn tightened her fist to quell the emotions bubbling up inside of her. She felt the opposite to Fleta; if she were forced to divert her attention, lower her guard, her feelings would eat her up. They'd been banished, she'd never see her parents again, Addison had left her, and now Bronson was missing. She was a mess, but the fear and loneliness that initially washed over her had turned into anger, especially at the way Addison had treated her. Her chest had tightened, and she had barely noticed Fleta and Kenley disappearing into the forest in front of her.

She headed to the river's edge. She needed to splash some cool water over her face to get herself focused. Fleta was her best friend, and Bronson had been a friend to her for as long as she knew; she needed to be there for them even if it meant packaging up all the turmoil building within her and putting them aside for the time being. She wanted to give herself this half-hour, to resolve all her pent-up feelings to a stage where she could pack them away, but they were overwhelming her.

At the edge of the river, she knelt on some pebbles that had settled upon the inside bank of a large sweeping bend in the river's flow. Cupping the cool water in her hand, she splashed it over her face, then rubbed it over her close-cut dark hair, savouring the cool sensation. She tried to put aside her feelings about Addison, but they were too strong to let go. How they'd last spoken filled her with guilt, anger and remorse. She allowed the memory to replay within her mind.

"If you want to stay, then stay! If you want to go, then go! I'm not the group's father; I couldn't give a shit," he'd said before throwing his arms up and walking beyond the clearing.

She'd chased after him.

"Addison, wait!" He stopped and turned to her, "You need to be better than this."

His brow collapsed into a series of deep ravines. Some were comically trapping his matted orange hair.

"You know, I thought you were coming over to take back what you said about forcing me into the 'leader' role, but you just chased me down to what? Double-down on it?"

"Do you honestly think anyone in this group has what it takes to get us to where we need to go? We've got a prissy princess with Wendy; someone who gets more pleasure out of provoking others than calming them in Lawson; Piper, who I'm certain has never actually spoken to anyone but Wendy; Stokely, who spends more time trying to appear invisible; Bronson who is currently doubled over in pain from Inauron-knows what illness; Fleta who is beside herself with grief; Kenley who hangs off Fleta's every word like a love-sick puppy; Corin who, unless the Book of Inauron has directions on where to go, is completely lost; and you, who has basically taken over his father's business and to whom Adair personally entrusted the directions to the lake. If you were me, who would you want looking after you?"

"You've forgotten someone," he crossed his arms and waited for her to figure it out.

The silence between them was deafening.

"Me?" She wasn't a leader, and nobody in that camp looked up to her like they did to Addison. He had their respect, whereas they all feared her temper.

"Bingo! You lead them. You talk about Adair's directions, but do you know what she actually said?" He waited for her in a faux-dramatic fashion, tilting his head and tapping at his elbow with his fingers nestled in the nook of his crossed arms. "Follow the river. There we go, now we both have all the information needed to get to the lake."

"I can't lead them; nobody looks up to me like they do to you."

"My entire life has just been upturned, and whilst I'm still trying to figure out what I still value in life, you're trying to push me into a role I don't want." He bit his lip, nervously. "Dawn; I'm hurting inside; I can't lead them."

"You don't need to wonder what to value," she said softly, warmly. "I'm right here."

"Are you?" He raised an eyebrow, "our betrothal was a business move by our parents, so we now have no obligation to continue this relationship."

"What?" She clenched her jaw, and her fingernails dug into the palms of her hands.

She basked in the silence, willing him to explain himself.

"Look," Addison immediately backtracked, "I shouldn't have said that; I'm sorry."

"That's how you feel? We're just business?"

"No, that's not it."

"You sounded pretty sure of yourself."

The propensity for arguments that had defined much of their relationship was out in full force, but Dawn wouldn't relent; he had crossed a line.

"I've been thinking a lot since we left the Grove. Do you still love me, or were you doing this out of obligation to your parents?" He cut her off before she responded, "because if it's the latter, we can part now, no hard feelings."

"Let me ask you a question, do you love me?" Dawn said through gritted teeth. "Have the past four years meant nothing?"

"I love you, Dawn. I can't deny that, even with how much we argue. We've never addressed how our relationship started and how important our parents' influence was in our love for each other. All the love we've built is real; I want you to know it is real," he punctuated his words with a chopping motion upon his other open palm. "But it's built on a shaky foundation that has just fallen apart, and we need to decide whether our love is strong enough to get through this. The one thing that tied us together - our parents - now matters no more."

She'd felt as though the wind had left her sails... everything within her just stopped.

"This may be the most hurt I've ever felt."

"Oh, stop, please," he said with an exasperated sigh. "Let's have an honest conversation about our relationship without all the theatrics."

She struck him; it wasn't enough for her to have her entire life pulled out from under her, but now the only thing that offered her some semblance of stability and security was getting cold feet and, on top of that, insulting her. She felt sick, and the fire burning inside her could not be quelled.

She looked at him with such vitriol that was ready to bite at him with another cutting argument, but the moment their eyes met, she realised what she'd done.

He held his face, water collected in the corner of his right eye, caused by the sting in his cheek.

"Get away from me," he said coldly.

She protested, but he raised his finger to stop her, saying, "I need to cool off; I can't continue this conversation with you."

He crossed a line, sure, but then she crossed an even bigger one as if they were inadvertently testing each other's boundaries. She'd won; she'd made him backtrack; if this were a war, the enemy would be routed, but the reality of what she'd done came crashing back down upon her, and she fell to her knees on the soft, moss-covered forest floor, tears welling up in her eyes.

She battled with a confusing and contradictory set of emotions. He'd made her do this, but she should never have done it. He was crying out for help, but she'd hit him instead of holding him. He behaved as if he were the only one in the group that mattered, but then to her, he *was* the only one that mattered. It was his fault, but she had started this argument and ended it. She was angry at him, but guilt washed over her. What had she turned into?

"He who gave us strength to fight for our lives," she whispered the passage from the Book of Inauron as it comforted her in times of difficulty. She knew they'd survive this if they fought for each other, but that doesn't mean they'd ever go back to normal, or go back to how they were. They were destined to fight for their lives forever-more in an endless cycle of ire.

As a couple, they had such a history of fiery arguments that the Devoted had, on more than one occasion, had to mediate. Though given their young age, it was often put down to nothing more than teenage emotions, which everyone goes through and eventually outgrows... If, of course, they survive the tribulations those emotions put upon them.

Addison turned to see her aground, "don't be surprised if this is the last time you see me."

She watched helplessly as he walked away into the forest, disappearing amongst the trees. In truth, she hadn't believed his words, but he had been right, he hadn't returned for the rest of the day, and that was the last she had seen of her love.

Still kneeling at the bank of the river, Dawn had closed her eyes; she was willing away the negative thoughts, attempting to ground herself at the moment else the moment would swallow her up.

At that point, she heard a cry coming from the opposite bank of the river, and so her eyes snapped open to identify the source. Immediately following the sound, she heard a splash. She could see the opposite bank; the river was only a few strides wide, but she couldn't see from where the sound was coming.

Sounds within the Wildlands were a phenomenon unto themselves; you couldn't trust your ears. The way the sound ricocheted between the trees of the dense forest, ravines and verges, you could perceive a sound as being directly ahead of you despite it being emitted from behind. She stood and leaned over the water to see the banks stretching to her left and right.

Upriver, she saw something floating towards her.

She immediately thought of Bronson, so without a second thought, she waded in as it flowed towards her. It was a person, face-down, floating like driftwood. She opened her arms, capturing him and lifting him as she struggled to pull him towards the bank.

As she stepped out of the water, she felt

the weight of her maroon, woollen gown pulling down on her body; it was not a material that was made for getting wet. Though with the weight of the dress was the added weight of the man she was pulling along with her; he was fully clothed in grey and soaked too. Despite this, Dawn found that the strength came easy to her; call it panic or adrenaline, but she lugged the prone form to the shore with impossible ease.

"Fleta, Kenley, I think I found him!" She yelled at the top of her lungs.

She turned over the figure before her, but it was not a face she knew.

It wasn't Bronson.

He, whoever he was, began to cough and splutter for breath.

7

Crossed Paths

It was approaching half an hour since Fleta and Kenley had left Dawn by the riverside. Since then, both trackers had found separate trails to follow until they could determine Bronson's correct path. It was the only time since the inferno some nights past that Kenley had had time away from the group, and like a wave, the worry came crashing into him.

He'd learned everything about tracking from his father, one of the town's foremost hunters; tracking was his most valuable skill. He knew the others wouldn't question his abilities because of the acclaim of his father's skills. Still, he worried that in trying to remain positive and confident in the face of Fleta's obvious distress; he had over-committed beyond that which he was truly capable - he couldn't bear the thought of her in pain. He began to second-guess himself, especially now that Fleta was alone, using only the teaching he'd given her to try and find her brother's trail. What if she became lost? Hurt?

He steadied himself on a tree as the panic rose within him. A throbbing began at his temples, emanating to the space behind his eyes. He shook himself free and tried to focus on the task at hand - the faster they found Bronson, the faster they could all relax, and he could drop this charade of being a tracker.

Jessil Coyde, Kenley's father, was known throughout the village as a hunter; he had two loves in his life, hunting first and Kenley's mother second. Jessil started as a model father, doting on his son as any proud father might. His profession saw him take long excursions away from the family home on the quiet outskirts of Penny Grove, close to the northern tree line. The Grove was named for its sizeable but hilly clearing almost entirely ringed by the trees of the Wildlands. It wouldn't be a stretch to say that The Grove itself was within the Wildlands since the great forest's trees reached out from its main body and wrapped themselves around the town. To the northwest of Penny Grove was the main trade route. This pathway took you towards Orenide Hills in the north, but also veered to the northeast, where Wenda's Rook sat at the foot of the Rooscane Mountains. Here, amongst the trees of the northern Wildlands and the rolling plains between Orenide Hills and Wenda's Rook, was where Kenley's father spent much of his time.

Jessil's attitude towards his son changed when he returned from a hunting trip to find Kenley, still but a babe, in his mother's arms, who had passed on during the night. One of his two loves was taken from him, and Jessil never recovered.

As Kenley grew older and saw other fathers playing with their children, he began questioning his father's ability to be an effective parent. He provided for Kenley, always ensuring he was cared for physically, but the emotional void that made up much of his father had not healed, and there was seemingly no place for Kenley within his heart. It wasn't until he grew older that he began to recognise what his father was going through. Still, despite this knowledge, Kenley wanted more than anything to gain his father's approval.

So he began reading his father's books and notes that he'd taken during his many hunting excursions, times in which he'd stay at the Ruthand household with Addison until he returned. Kenley devoured these books; his father kept detailed logs of his hunts and journeys. He was confident that he knew everything there was to learn academically about tracking and hunting - the practical experience was all that he was lacking. Kenley had never so much as set foot beyond the trees into the Wildlands until their exile.

This lack of experience was the spear that jabbed at his conscience. The same question came up repeatedly in his thoughts - is simply *knowing how* to track in this terrain enough to do this for real?

He'd been walking and following a trail for nearly half an hour before he became convinced he was on the right course. Four evenings ago, after their banishment, the area had experienced light but constant rainfall. The weather had cleared since then, producing mud that was supple enough to show clear footprints, not just mere suggestions. There was one such footprint, clearly pressed into the earth, with minimal forestry residue atop it. This meant that not only was it a clear sign of a trail, but it was also proof of recency. It was the golden egg of tracking; a sign that none could doubt.

His emotions heightened at the realisation that his efforts had not been in vain; elation, relief, and joy. As the feelings reached their apex, he felt an enormous weight overpower his body. He fell to a knee, then his eyes rolled back, his neck tensing to reveal the tendons and blood vessels. The pain that had started as a throb behind his eyes, blossomed into white, hot excruciating anguish, and he fought it with all his might. He couldn't let this pain delay him; the thought of Fleta not reuniting with her brother lit a fire under him, and he pushed through the pain, grasping a low tree branch to stabilise himself as he returned to his feet. With deep breaths, the pain began to subside, and his muscles relaxed, returning his body back to normal.

A voice he recognised called out.

"Kenley?"

* * *

Fleta was sick to her stomach; almost every breath sickened her as if the morning's air was toxic. She knew it was worry. Her hope that her struggles were behind her were cruelly dashed with Bronson's disappearance. Just as she started to relax and savour her uncle's absence, Bronson had taken off without a word. She endeavoured to stick to her task; she had to find him. She hoped her worry would take a back seat by diverting all her attention to the hunt. Unrealistic this may be, but it was all she had. So she scanned the undergrowth for signs of his passage.

Kenley had opted to go alone for a short while, and they would meet back at the riverside once they could either confirm Bronson's track or at least check a track off their list. There were many interconnected game trails littering the forest, snaking around and crossing over one another in a disorganised manner. It was the reason they lost his track to begin with.

As she walked, Fleta nibbled at her nails and chewed at the dead skin around them - it was one of her many comfort habits; she wouldn't say it gave her relief, but what it did well was distract her. She had grown up in a hostile environment and bore many scars and idiosyncrasies because of her hardships. She tasted blood beneath one of her fingernails, a bitter metallic taste. Kenley had just been trying to wake her. Her method of distraction from her worry had yet yielded another separate fear - will Kenley ever trust her after that?

She didn't have a history with Kenley to speak of, they'd all but moved in different circles as they grew up, but the last day or so had shown him in a new light. He always seemed to be near when she needed something, be it water, fire-tending, collecting firewood or cooking with the scant supplies they'd brought. Taking care of Bronson and comforting Dawn the previous day had taken her total mental capacity. She was grateful for Kenley's help in propping her up and ensuring they were all well cared for.

When she'd scratched him, she worried that all the goodwill they'd built had disintegrated. With this worry, her mind wandered, and the single-mindedness she'd cultured to find her brother evaporated, taking with it the knowledge of the current trail she occupied. She couldn't remember the last clue, or the one before it.

She wrung her hands together; her long, thick, dark hair blew into her face by a passing breeze, obscuring her vision, and her breath shortened. By instinct, she closed her eyes and took herself to a place of comfort, fields of daisies swaying in a cool, calming breeze, a warm sun casting a glow across her relaxed body. It was a defence mechanism, a place she took herself when she had no place else to go, a place in a world which was uniquely hers. Her childhood trauma had impacted her ability to be close to others but had enhanced her imagination. On command, she could conjure worlds and teleport herself into them emotionally, distancing herself from any physical sensations she may be experiencing.

Once she'd calmed her nerves, she slowly returned to her physical surroundings and found herself sat at the foot of a moss-ridden tree. She had tucked herself in a nook surrounded by the arcing roots of an enormous oak in its waning years. She took a deep breath, feeling the rest of the worry slip away into nothingness; a shudder ran down her spine in response.

She spied a clear footprint near her outstretched legs, and warmth flooded her; she was on the right track. She would find her brother; this was the sign she sought. She had proof that he'd passed this way and could finally look forward to the prospect of holding him again.

The feeling was short-lived, as a desperate cry cut the forest's silence from nearby. Leaves rustled, an audible struggle, a thump as something hit the ground, and someone cried out in pain. Fleta got to her feet and cut through the trees to find its source. A short distance away through the brush, she saw Kenley with one knee in the dirt, eyes rolling back into his skull, his face contorted into an ugly grimace, tears dripping down his face as he fought whatever was ailing him. She closed the gap between them just as he regained his awareness and rose to his feet.

"Kenley?" She cried out, concern in her eyes.

She was met with silence, so she worried he hadn't heard her; just as she opened her mouth to address him once more, he replied, "Fleta? What are you doing here?"

"Never mind that; what the hell? Are you

okay?"

He was breathless but mustered a reply, "yes, it was a headache, I think."

"Don't downplay it; I've had plenty of headaches but none like that!"

"It's plagued me since this morning, but it's never this bad, normally just a dull throb."

He could see the concern in her eyes, so he quickly elaborated, "it's gone away as quickly as it arrived. Really, I'm fine now."

He stood and shook off the remaining struggle, wiping at the stream of involuntary tears that stained his face.

She let the silence sit, unable to grasp what she'd seen of him. A silence that he then broke.

"I found a footprint!"

"What? So did I!"

"Facing which direction?"

She pointed north, in the same direction as the footprint he found.

"Show me," he said, his brow furrowed.

Fleta led him back through the foliage some distance and pointed at the footprint; she was proud of herself and beamed a grin in his direction, feeling the relief that she was finally on track to finding Bronson. Kenley, however, didn't seem to share her delight. He raised his arms, interlocking his hands atop his scalp and winced.

"What is it?"

"I..." He stuttered, struggling to find the words.

"We're not alone out here."

Fleta's stomach dropped, and the nausea of worry regained prominence in her body. Not alone... The stories they'd all been taught as children were that the Wildlands were uninhabited. None of them had considered that they'd find others out here, living amongst the tress. She needed more information to stop the sickness rising.

"How do you mean?"

"This footprint differs from the one I found; different size, different tread impression, but this also looks like it was made recently."

She thought about what this might mean when a cold shock reddened her cheeks, "oh no, Dawn! We left her alone, what if these people find her?"

"Shit, let's go!" Kenley held out his arm to direct her to move ahead of him, and they ran as quickly as the dense undergrowth would allow them, back towards the river's edge.

They leapt across fallen logs, slipped on muddy earth, and cut through the brush to return to Dawn. Fleta's heart pounded; her propensity to worry was in overdrive. She imagined the worst; Dawn was lost, no Dawn was hurt, Dawn was being murdered right then; she couldn't stop the thoughts from attacking her. She needed to be grounded and return to the riverside to confirm that Dawn was okay. Each immediate need clawed for priority within her until she became weary.

Then, she noticed she was running alone; Kenley had fallen back. As she stopped, an almost paralysing fear spread through her; Dawn was taken, Bronson was lost, and now Kenley was missing.

She was alone.

She was afraid.

Kenley's familiar cry brought her back to reality, and she quickly moved towards the sound. Again she found him on his knees; this time, his head pointed skyward, his eyeballs were completely white, and his neck strained so hard that she could see the blood pumping to his face. His skin was darkening; his normally unblemished, tanned brown complexion now had a greyness to it she found alarming. His arms flailed out beside him, his fingers tensed, fixed into an almost unnatural claw. He fell backwards and writhed in the dirt, kicking up soil and leaves; his head moved from side to side as he fought against the pain, mixing his dark curls with the detritus of the forest floor. Blood dripped from his ears, then his nose, then the sides of his eyes; he let out a morbid cry for reprieve, until finally, he fell silent.

8

A Vision Most Unnatural

Kenley saw much within his mind at the point he fell unconscious. His vision left his body on the ground and climbed skyward, still pointing at his contorted but now silent form. Fleta crouched over him, trying to wake him up.

"Please wake up, Kenley," she cried, "I don't want to be left alone; I need you."

Before he could react, he suddenly found himself flying across the forest at breakneck speed until he stared at three stone statues. They were humanoid in form but different somehow. There were two adults, a supposed man and wife, and a child. The statues were old, and he couldn't tell whether the peculiarities in their appearances were intentional or a result of ages of erosion. As he took in the scene, he saw an approach from the north.

"What the hell are these things?" Lawson said.

"Weird," Wendy said, clasping Lawson's hand in a familiar embrace. "You think they want to watch us?"

Wendy smirked at Lawson, raising a flirtatious eyebrow.

"Of course they want to watch," Lawson chuckled, "who wouldn't."

Before the scene could play out in front of him, he saw a flash, advancing the scene ahead in time, and it was only visible for a few moments, but what he saw chilled him to the bone.

Lawson was strung up between two trees, his nude body on display for all to see, and he was riddled with cuts. Blood was running down his body and dripping into a large stone bowl beneath him. The child statue was alive, making more cuts on him with a piece of obsidian, causing a rivulet of blood to dribble over his skin and down to the bowl. He screamed in agony as the statue placed a piece of stone in the gap within his now-open flesh, forcing the artery open further. The father and mother statues were close by; the father held a stone shafted spear tipped with obsidian, and the mother stood over the bowl that collected Lawson's blood as she chanted in some forgotten tongue.

The scene's horror was palpable, but he was prevented from reacting, as his vision took to the skies of the forest once more. He saw Addison, who ran through the woods as if pursued by an unknown assailant; draped across his arms was the corpse of Corin. Her skin was grey, drained of life, and she bore a sickening wound upon her head. She looked cold, and her stiff, broken pose sickened Kenley. Addison's face was etched with fear as he approached a small hut adorned in the hanging bones of various animals; an orchestra of death played as the wind blew through the clearing knocking against the hanging talismans and wind-chimes of bone, feather and leathern flesh.

Flying further afield, he saw Dawn with the bodies of four men aground in front of her. Her fists were clenched, blood dripped, and anger seared her face. The bodies were all wearing grey robes with a small gold symbol on the breast that he couldn't quite make out... for they were splattered with gore. One's head was nearly detached entirely from his neck, another bore scratch marks so deep they looked as though four separate blades had made them, another's face was mangled and pulped into a hardly recognisable form, and the other's body lay facing up, whilst his face was impossibly looking into the dirt behind him with a swollen, twisted neck. Despite the gore and the horror, what scared him most was Dawn's expression. It made his blood run cold. One would typically struggle to see the relationship between an unassuming, diminutive form as Dawn and the sheer violence of the scene in front of her. Still, because of her grimace alone, Kenley knew that she'd done this.

His vision moved again, flying back to Penny Grove. He saw Fleta, straddling a prone form, her expression blank as the fire-poker she grasped landed across her victim's face again and again and again. Her expression was like a mannequin, static and unchanging, seemingly oblivious to the spray of hot blood across it.

Once more, the vision flashed, leaping to the town square. Grey-robed men lined the streets, and the townsfolk were herded like sheep into the town hall opposite the carcass of the Sanctuary. He could hear Councillor Adair's voice attempt to calm the citizenry as they panicked. The door was locked behind them, and the building began to burn around them. Screams echoed into the night, but the grey-robed men outside faced away as they burned.

This scream was the catalyst that caused the vision to move once more, and he found himself back where his body lay on the forest floor, with Fleta at his side, and as his vision slowly approached his prone form, his eyes flicked open, and he awoke.

9

Cottonmouth

The worst thing Bronson experienced with this withdrawal sickness wasn't the constant cottonmouth or the throbbing headache. It was the damned voices just at the edge of his hearing all around him, not loud enough for him to recognise but not quiet enough to drown out; a constant background chatter. He was desperate for the volume to either increase to allow him to hear the voices more clearly or decrease to leave him with his peace. The drone of voices modulated its volume occasionally, but never to the level where he could hear what it was saying. In truth, he doubted that he was even hearing voices, but that seemed to be the closest approximation of the sounds.

Gravel is a hallucinogenic high, making the

user see, hear and feel things that aren't there, and the withdrawal from gravel seemed like the drug's last hurrah before it left his system for good. At its best, some things in the forest appeared to be slightly different in colour than they should be, or making a somewhat different sound than expected, but at its worst, he saw things that didn't exist.

He'd followed Javi from their makeshift camp to the river, but as is customary with his Uncle, the five-minute journey to the river and back quickly turned into a long trek through the woods. Javi insisted that he find himself some mushrooms of the same variety used to make gravel.

"They're not potent enough to give you a high, but they'll sure as shit take the edge off your withdrawal," his uncle told him. His sickness from the withdrawal was pronounced enough for him to be physically and emotionally drained; he wanted nothing more than for the sickness to end. So Bronson stepped behind his dishevelled uncle as he followed his nose through the thickets and brush.

He was apprehensive about leaving his sister and Dawn behind, but his current journey chemically outweighed those feelings in his mind; he needed this withdrawal to end so that he could be there for them; this journey was a means to an end.

He thought briefly of his sister, who, since leaving Penny Grove finally felt like his sister again, not the hollowed husk of a person who had occupied her body these past few years. At the thought, he wept; his tears were unexpected but not altogether unwelcome; he needed it. He was so drained that he hadn't the inclination nor energy to stop the feelings from spilling out of him.

"Th'fuck's up with you?" Javi said.

Bronson tried to compose himself by wiping at his eyes, "oh nothing, don't worry about it."

"Hell of a withdrawal, eh?"

"I just want it to end."

Javi slapped him on the back in a clumsy attempt at comfort.

"We'd best find some of these mushrooms then, hadn't we? I would have picked some up on my way out here, but you guys had already given me a healthy head-start and I didn't want to waste time."

Before he knew it, he was back on his uncle's heels as Javi pushed on through the forest, determined to find some of the elusive hallucinogens.

They grew copiously near Penny Grove, but deep in the Wildlands, the vegetation was different, and the biodiversity exceptional. There were trees tall enough for a layer of mist within the forest to obscure the visibility of their uppermost canopies, the light cast mote-lit beams through the air, and there seemed to be more layers of distinct vegetation than he'd ever known.

The bottom-most layer was filled with mosses, decaying leaves and fallen trees, providing ample nutrients to seedlings that sprouted up; atop this, there were fungi, small shrubs, bushes and other low-lying plants, following were the larger bushes that sometimes reached up to the mid-point of the many tree trunks, some of this vegetation dwarfed him in comparison. Despite it being the middle of the day, so many shadows were cast that one could be forgiven for assuming it was twilight.

His Uncle had allegedly followed the group from the village through the night, then found himself lost, before finally happening upon their encampment by chance. He'd stayed hidden until Bronson became separated from the others, and it was then that he'd jumped in to help his nephew recover from withdrawal.

"Couldn't have brought any gravel with you, could you?" Bronson had asked him, expecting him to bring at least a few stones.

"Gotta teach you kids to fend for yourselves, haven't I?" he'd retorted. "Ain't always gonna be around."

Bronson collapsed onto a fallen log, placing

his head in his hands.

"Come on, mate," Javi said. His uncle's dark, messy hair had forest detritus caught within its strands, and his face wore the evidence of days without shaving. Other than that, Javi looked as he always did, sneering at anything appearing even remotely weak.

"Just give me a few minutes to clear my head," the constant drone of voices-or-not-voices was overwhelming him. He willed them away but had no strength, and there were too many different noises to deal with; it was as if he was trying to catch a single fly in the middle of a swarm.

The cottonmouth was intense and unwavering. Bronson had drunk gallons of water from the river they passed, but it couldn't avail him of his discomfort. He felt as though his entire body was vibrating as he rested his head in his hands, which couldn't contain their trembling. He couldn't let this go on.

"I'll stay here; you go find the mushrooms," he told his uncle.

"No way, you're coming too."

"Javi, I can't," Bronson protested, "I can barely move, let alone think, let alone search."

"You're overreacting now," Javi replied with more distaste.

"I don't think I am; I need help."

Javi took Bronson under his arm and tried to lift him, whilst Bronson, in turn, planted himself to the log as tightly as his body allowed.

"Get off me," he yelled at his uncle.

"Then make me," Javi yelled back.

Bronson grabbed at his uncle's hands which wrapped under his arm, unable to free the grip that was lifting him from the log.

"Come on, you lazy prick," Javi taunted. "You want to stay there; you must fight me for the privilege."

Bronson sneered at him and began jostling his arms back and forth to shake the older, more muscular man's grip from him.

Javi pulled Bronson up and over, causing the boy to land on the detritus that covered the ground.

"What the hell, why are you doing this?" Bronson said.

"No reason," Javi replied, pointing near Bronson's head, at the patch of mushrooms that spread out in front of them.

Javi cackled with glee as Bronson realised this had all been a big joke to him. Javi picked some and began eating the caps straight from the stalk as if they were food from a market stall in the village fair. Bronson quickly rolled over and did the same, slowly getting to his feet as he ate the mushrooms like they were the only thing he'd eaten in weeks.

Within minutes, the feelings from the withdrawal faded; the headache, the cottonmouth, the disorientation. He drank deeply from a water skin he'd filled at the river, washing down the earthy taste of the mushrooms. They tasted far more bitter when eaten raw, but he didn't care; he knew he had to do this quickly and get back to his sister.

He began picking up more to store for later when he noticed the voices hadn't quieted. He'd almost become used to them and, in his frenzy over the mushrooms, they had moved to the back of his attention. When he realised the noise was still present, it rushed back to the forefront of his focus.

They were louder somehow but still indistinct. There was a single voice he could make out, one he tried hard to centre on because it felt familiar to him. Still without discernible words, he focused firmly; it sounded like Fleta. He reminded himself of his sister's voice as he recalled her comforting him during his sickness, and at that moment, the indistinct voice became as apparent as if he were standing next to her.

"Please wake up, Kenley," she cried, "I don't want to be left alone; I need you."

"Fleta?" Bronson asked, confused.

"Bronson?" Fleta replied.

Bronson shot to his feet and looked around to find his sister, but he couldn't see her.

"You can hear me?"

"Where are you, Bron?" She sounded upset in her reply; he recognised how her voice trembled. He thought he could feel which direction the disembodied voice came from, and he turned to face it.

"I'm here with Javi," he said. He waved his hands about, "can you see me?"

"No, you're not, Bron, you're not with Javi. There's nobody around me but Kenley, and he's..." she didn't finish her sentence.

"What's happened?" His voice became louder as he sensed her unease.

"I need you Bron, where are you? Please come back to me."

He took steps towards where the sound was coming from.

"I'll come to you; I think I know which way - I'll bring Javi with me."

"You can't bring Javi with you, Bron."

"What do you mean, course I can; we're on our way," he said, concern written in furrows across his brow.

"No Bronson, you're not listening to me; you can't bring Javi with you..." she paused. "...because he's dead."

Bronson looked back to where Javi stood to find himself alone in the forest. A sickening feeling spread throughout his body. Was Javi part of his withdrawal, or was this voice part of his withdrawal? He couldn't tell, and his heart pounded as he tried to make sense of his surroundings.

He had no option; he had to follow the voice.

"I'm on my way," he said.

10

Brother

"You must excuse me," the man began, "I don't have the warmest experiences with others met within the Wildlands."

Dawn had lifted him from the water with strength she didn't realise she had, desperate to rescue who she thought was Bronson. The freshly revived man sat on the pebbles with a heavy, sodden cloak about his shoulders.

"Who are you?" Dawn asked; she looked the man up and down and noted his attire, the plain grey robe, the golden embroidered symbol of a tree within a circular wrapping of branches at his breast.

"I am Brother Yuri, and I am... or rather *was*, a Devotee of the Sanctuary at Wenda's Rook up north." She found it concerning that he never caught her gaze or seemed to wonder about his surroundings. He was elderly, in his seventies at least, with hair as white as a daisy and thin skin that seemed to lose all its adherence to his bones, placing worry lines all across his face. Adorning his face was a significant red mark that crossed his face from his right-side forehead to his left-side cheek; it was beginning to bruise at his brow and the bridge of his nose.

"I'm Dawn." She wondered how much to tell this strange man of their circumstances but determined to keep it simple. "We're from Penny Grove, and a friend of ours has got himself lost in these woods, and we're trying to track him."

The man grumbled under his breath before finally recognising that he should perhaps share his thoughts with Dawn. "Lost in the Wildlands… You'd be safer to return to your town."

"What do you mean?" She pressed.

"I'm sorry, it's been a long time since I've spoken with another; I'm somewhat out of practice; much of my words manage to stay within my mind, or worse, get spoken aloud when they should have stayed in my mind." Dawn waited for him to elaborate though his words were slow and soft, "anyone who gets lost out here becomes lost not just physically, but also in spirit. Something about the wilds around here captures them, and they can't escape. It's like a spider's web; it seems simple at first, you can practically trace your finger along the surface to chart your comings and goings, but the moment you sit on the silk, you can't get yourself back out."

He looked listlessly at a single point above her whilst he spoke; it was disconcerting; it felt almost as though the words he was saying were rehearsed, and that, on top of responding to her question, he also had to recall the exact words from deep within a memory bank.

"How did you end up in the river," she asked, unintentionally beginning to interrogate the man from the river.

"Would you believe I fell?"

"I heard a scream,"

"Me, I'm afraid." He looked embarrassed, "at my age, losing my footing is common. I'm not sure you've noticed, but I'm mostly blind."

It finally dawned on her that she had mistaken his blindness for something more sinister with the listless gaze and the lack of eye contact. Her suspicion had been for naught.

"I'm sorry."

"What for, child?"

"Your blindness." He opened his mouth to soothe her, but she clarified her meaning before he could, "I had you pegged as a liar."

"Oh, a liar I may still be," he smirked, "but I'm also blind."

He broke into a deep laugh that ended in the coughing and spluttering she'd heard moments before. She couldn't help but share his gaiety, despite the circumstances.

"What's a Devotee of the Sanctuary doing in the Wildlands?"

"Ah, that's a terribly long story. I've been banished, you see, and I don't know why. I suspect its something someone thought I saw, so they took my sight and sent me out here."

"That's terrible; I'm sorry to hear that, Brother."

"I did introduce myself as 'Brother', did I not? It would perhaps be more pertinent to call me Yuri, since my banishment was also an excommunication of-sorts. In truth, I've been out here for nearly thirty years, wandering through these dense Wildlands. I'm firmly at their mercy."

"Thirty years!" Dawn exclaimed, unable to comprehend how it was possible to live in this land that had been so hostile to them since they arrived. "How have you survived with your condition?"

"I generally stay in one place; I have a small hut not far from here - I grow my own food and stay close to the river for water. It's not that difficult." He thought momentarily, anticipating some of the questions she may have, "You see, when you're blind, distances become a series of countable steps rather than a visual thing, if you will. It becomes something you learn and mentally map out."

"How do you keep yourself from bumping into trees? The forest is unusually dense here."

Yuri doubled back and laughed loudly, and as his glee began to subside, he began to answer.

"You know, that's a pretty good question now that I think about it. I used a long stick that I waved back and forth to ensure I walked safely. However, I haven't needed it for quite some time, as I'm pretty confident around my hut." He chuckled once more before returning to a more serious tone, "though, since my tumble into the river, I must confess that I am truly lost now."

"Can I help?" Dawn asked. "I have to wait for my friends to return, but once they do, I can guide you back to your hut."

"I can't go back there," he said suddenly and sharply, almost cutting her off.

Dawn reverted to her earlier assumption about Yuri's character - he was hiding something from her. She gazed across the river where the sound of his falling had originated, trying to see through the greens, greys and browns on the opposite bank to find something worthy of an explanation.

Sensing her unease at his comment, Yuri started, stumbling a little before regaining his confidence in his words, "I... I think it's time I moved on from there. This place... I think I've been lucky to stay hidden these past years. Now though... I'm not so hidden."

"What does that mean?" Dawn questioned.

"I simply need some help relocating."

He placed the tip of his finger into his mouth and raised it into the breeze to detect the direction of the wind. He then brought his arm down, pointing somewhat southwest.

"There," he said. "Around ten minutes walk this way, I have put aside a small cache of belongings to help me navigate the forest; a new stick, some fresh clothes, some food. I've prepared for this."

Dawn felt a cold shiver; whatever Yuri was escaping from clearly posed a danger to her and her friends, so why was he so mysterious? Is this what happened to Bronson? Had he been attacked or taken by whatever Yuri fears?

"I'll help you." She thought momentarily, "But you must tell me what you're running from."

A twig snap from the east startled her, and her eyes shot to where the sound came from, across the river.

Her eyes searched the brush and the trees for movement, but she could only see trees, leaves, and branches. Though as she looked, she centred in on a confusing shape, at first she could not determine what it was; it was grey and large. She'd initially mistaken it for some boulder, but as she looked deeper, she noticed the eyes atop it almost buried within a mass of dark hair, with a gaze fixed upon hers.

Her blood ran cold.

They were being watched.

"Someone is watching us." She whispered, shivers running down her spine.

Yuri lowered his head into his hands. "They've found me, then."

"Who's found you?" Dawn asked, panic rising.

"Please help me up; I must go to my cache. There's no time to wait."

Unable to think for herself, Dawn rushed to his aid, helping him up from the ground, his clothes still wet, causing him to hunch with the added weight.

"Who is it?" She asked him, this time with more urgency.

"I don't wish to expose you to my history; it's simply better that you take me to my cache and then find a place to hide. It is my demon, my mistake to live with."

"Are my friends in danger? If they return here whilst I'm helping you, are they at risk?"

He shrugged. "I can only lead them away and hope for the best…"

11

Long Awaited Embrace

Kenley's eyes opened to the blinding light of the forest. His heart pounded as he recalled the visions that had flooded him moments before; so much death, so much pain; Lawson's bloodcurdling screams, Corin's deathly grimace, Dawn's demented stare, the men in grey sprawled about in the forest, Fleta's empty gaze, and at The Grove their loved ones being burned alive in the coffin of the town-hall. It all felt so real; not just a bad dream. He needed to feel something physical to snap himself out of his stupor, so his hands grasped at the surrounding ground, feeling the texture of the mosses and detritus that carpeted the forest floor.

His eyes finally adjusted to the world around him; he could see Fleta close by, pacing. It looked like she was talking to herself; he strained to hear.

"You can't bring Javi with you, Bron," he heard her say. Was she talking to her brother? Kenley sat up slightly and looked around; she hadn't noticed him yet, but he couldn't see her wayward brother anywhere. She talked as if to herself, not to a person. Her eyes and head were not directed at any location that would give Kenley a clue as to where Bronson was.

"No, Bronson, you're not listening to me; you can't bring Javi with you...," she paused, "...because he's dead."

He's dead.

Her uncle was dead.

His vision replayed in his head. Fleta straddling a body, blood spraying across her face.

His blood ran cold.

He had an overwhelming urge to learn more, disprove the visions' reality, and feel comfortable knowing that what he saw was no more than a bad dream. But, he knew that if he were to ask, there was a chance she could validate them. He felt sick, but he had to know.

"Your uncle is dead?"

His voice startled her, and she fell to the ground as she screamed, clutching her hands at her chest.

"Oh, you're awake," she said, panting as she

realised she was not in danger. "I'm sorry; I didn't mean to get scared like that."

"Is he dead?" Kenley asked again.

She paused, looking across at anywhere but him. They were both planted firmly on the ground across from one another. She finally met his eyes.

"Yes."

"Was it you?"

The pause was long. Painful. He could see the difficulty posed by his question in her eyes as she battled with herself.

"Yes."

He had one more question to ask, and it was the one that scared him the most. It was a question that could give credence to the vision, proving it was real, or could finally make him put aside the fanciful dream as just a side-effect of his excruciating episode.

"With a fire poker?"

She paled at the question, unable to answer. She stammered a little as her mouth struggled to form words. He watched as her face leapt through many emotions, surprise, terror, and confusion.

She finally answered.

"Yes."

He inhaled and fell back onto the ground,

eyes pointed to the heavens.

"How do you know?" Her question wasn't accusatory; it was genuine.

"I saw it..."

She furrowed her brow and gave an expression that he interpreted as both horror and confusion simultaneously. She didn't speak, so he continued.

"... Just now. I saw it a moment ago. A vision. I had hoped it was a bad dream, but now..."

"What do you mean?"

"Oh, Fleta, I saw some horrible things. All of us, and everyone we know is in danger, or have already been in danger, or are about to be in danger, I can't tell." He couldn't stop the words from flowing. "One of the many confusing and violent things I saw was you atop your uncle, beating him. I had hoped it wasn't true, I hoped so hard, but if you truly did kill your uncle, then it means my vision wasn't a dream. It's real."

A tear fell down Fleta's cheek as she recalled the night of the fire and Javi's fate. It wasn't regret but an acknowledgement that she could no longer hide it; this was her burden.

"I hope you don't think less of me-" she started before he cut her off.

"For murdering your uncle with a fire poker?" His voice was louder than he intended, and he winced as he considered his volume. Bringing it back down, he continued, "how can I not?"

She wiped at the tears that were now freely flowing down her cheeks. Opening her mouth to speak, she found that no voice was forthcoming.

Kenley had always doted after Fleta, even if she hadn't realised it all these years. She had a significant place in his heart since they were young, but knowing that she had murdered her uncle changed things. It felt so out-of-character for her; at least it differed from the impression of her he had built up in his head. It made him realise just how little he knew of her. She could very well be a monster.

"You don't understand, Kenley," she started, but before she could continue to defend herself, she realised she didn't have the conviction. The considerable part of her life she'd kept sealed behind a locked door within her psyche was not ready to be opened.

"We should find Dawn," Kenley said, pulling himself up to his feet.

"I'm waiting for my brother."

"What do you mean waiting?"

"I talked to him."

"Well, where is he?"

"No, I talked to him; somehow, we talked to each other."

He wondered briefly if this was another

shadow of madness within her character; she murdered her uncle in cold blood and now talks to her brother over a seemingly great distance. Who on earth had he thrown his lot in with?

Over the last day or so, he and Fleta had grown closer. They'd shared camaraderie and seemed to enjoy each other's company when she wasn't caring for Bronson. It was what he'd always wanted; the love he felt for her finally seemed within reach of being reciprocated, but now, he didn't know what he wanted.

She sensed his unease over her words, "I know it sounds stupid. But it was him, and he is coming."

"I don't think we can afford to wait," He thought of Dawn covered in blood with the bodies of the grey-robed men beneath her, "I don't know what's to become of Dawn."

"Go then!" Her shout took him by surprise. "Get away from me if you're so scared."

He closed his eyes and admonished himself for having little faith in her. He felt paralysed. Torn between rescuing Dawn and rescuing Fleta and her brother. Sickness rose within him. He needed to decide right now, with no further delay.

"I'll wait with you."

The tears streamed down her face, and she brought her knees up to her chest, hiding her face behind them. The sight tugged at him, and his eyes filled with tears. Nothing about what he saw of her gave him any notion of her being a cold-blooded killer; he wished he could take back what he said.

He brushed himself off before settling back onto the ground next to her. He crossed his feet and nervously placed an arm around her to comfort her. She shrank under his touch, like a stray cat from the village who didn't want to be petted, and she shook his hand off her.

"Please don't touch me," she whispered through the tears.

"I'm sorry," he said quietly, "for how I reacted."

She didn't acknowledge his apology, but he continued talking anyway. He just wanted her to hear him.

"I saw horrifying things in that vision, which scared me." He swallowed, feeling a lump in his throat. Tapping at his temple, he said, "I'm afraid of everything that happened there."

Kenley's chest wavered, threatening to become hyperventilation.

"What I saw of you... the expression on your face upset me in a way I didn't expect, and I'm sorry for my reaction, I... wish I could take it back."

She pivoted her foot on her heel, placing her

boot against his. She didn't look up or give him any other sign she accepted his words. If that's all the physical contact she could muster, then that's what he would gladly accept.

They sat like that, without speaking, for what seemed like half an hour. He listened to her quiet breaths, erratic though they were with her sorrow, and looked down at his foot, with her boot against his. His ankle ached from the angle, but he wouldn't move his foot unless she did first; he didn't want to risk losing the only physical contact they'd ever had.

The minutes passed in silence, interrupted only by the wind cutting through the trees and the occasional hoot of an owl in the dim light. It felt like solace, the tiniest piece of comfort in an otherwise tumultuous situation. He thought more about her actions against her uncle; there had to be a reason, he must have missed something. He saw so little of the event in question, just two or three seconds, and he knew that couldn't be enough to judge someone over, even if it looked damning. He wanted to learn more and find out why she did it, but he could sense her unease and knew this wasn't the right time.

A rustling came through the bushes to the north, and he tensed at what it might be.

Pale and shorn of the head, Bronson marched through the undergrowth, scanning the surroundings for his sister. Before Kenley could call him over, Bronson raised his hands to his face and bellowed.

"Flea!"

He didn't even see Fleta move from beside him, he just felt a slight crackle, perhaps a rustling of the foliage and then she was in her brother's arms. He held her off the ground; her arms and legs were wrapped tightly around him.

"There you are," he said.

She didn't want to let him go; that much was clear.

"I'm here now; relax." He held her close and closed his eyes. Although they were twins, Kenley sensed it had been some time since they'd held each other like this. Bronson needed it just as much as Fleta did.

Slowly, she stepped back onto the ground and looked up at him, tears in her eyes. He met her gaze and leaned in close.

"I need you to tell me about Javi," he said.

12

Cast Iron Will

"I'm going to need you to help me," Bronson pleaded.
"What is it?"

"I won't have any gravel outside of the Grove - which means I'm going to withdraw as soon as it clears my system."

This was the most open he'd ever been about his gravel habit, it went unspoken, but both knew that the other knew enough. He'd never addressed it directly with her, and that in itself spoke volumes to the worry he felt. In order to ask her, he needed to overcome their animosity.

"What do you need me to do?"

"Javi and I cooked up a batch last night; it'll be dry, cracked and bagged up in the house, most likely on the mantelpiece above the hearth. Can you get it for me?"

"Why can't you get it?" She didn't want to be alone after this evening.

"I need to help our parents at the Sanctuary; there's still so much rubble in the streets. Every man is there; it'll look bad if I'm not."

"Okay, I'll go."

"Thank you, Flea," he leaned in to kiss her. "If I have a small supply, I can slowly wean myself off it without too much harm. You'll need to be in control of it, though."

She nodded and set off towards the house around the other side of the Sanctuary, avoiding the pools of water that collected in the townspeople's footprints in the slick mud. She could see people still rushing back and forth with pails, some from the river nearby, some from the well, to attempt to contain the blaze that had been raging for hours. Screams and shouts echoed around; some were commanding instructions, others were crying, or grieving. Seeing the townspeople she grew up around in so much pain was like a knife to the heart.

She did not know how the fire started; it wasn't there one moment, and then there it was, making its way up the tapestries to the roof. It was so uncontrollable that salvaging the situation themselves had never been possible.

Fleta pushed open the door into the house

and quickly looked around. The house was quiet, and as the door behind her closed and cut off the sound of the chaos outside, she found herself in an unsettling emptiness. The house was dark, with the last few flames dancing in their ailing hearth doing a poor job of lighting the room. She stood for a moment in the quiet darkness, listening intently, then breathed a sigh of relief when she realised she was alone.

Gingerly, she stepped around the furniture, careful not to trip in the long shadows cast by the dim hearth. She leaned over and reached for the small leather pouch atop the mantlepiece, but before her hand could grasp the bag, a hand shot from the shadows, taking her wrist firmly in its grip.

"Here for one last goodbye kiss, are you, love?" Javi said. Her heart jumped into her throat and she yelped. He was sitting there in the dark, shirking his responsibility to the town. She grimaced, immediately knowing what he wanted.

"Don't do this," she said. "Not now... I need the gravel for Bronson."

"I'll give you the gravel, sure," he said as he let her arm go and picked up the pouch. He tossed the bag in the air and caught it again, walking into the light from the fire to face her. She immediately smelled the Bark's Ale on his breath and it sickened her. It was a scent that was intrinsically tied to all those memories of abuse throughout her years. "It's all here. Do you want it?"

She reached for it, but he snatched it away at the last second.

"If you want the gravel, there's something you need to do for me," he said.

"No," she said firmly. "I won't do it."

"The gravel withdrawal is hell, y'know," he tossed the bag in the air again, snatching it out of the air before Fleta had any ideas of trying to intercept it. "Are you willing to let your brother go through that just because you don't want to give me what I want?"

"You make me sick."

"Now-now, there's no need for insults, just get on your knees, and I'll make this quick." He pushed on her shoulder towards the ground, he was far stronger than her, and despite her protest, she was forced to the floor onto her knees.

"You know what I want, and I know what you want," he said, whilst waving the pouch of gravel. "Remember... this isn't for me; this is for Bron, of course."

"I won't do it."

His expression changed quickly; his outward persona dissipated leaving in its ashes, the persona that she knew so well. Here, stood before her, with a sneer and a clenched fist, was the real Javi.

"Girl, you either do it and get the gravel, or I force you to do it anyway, and you don't get it. It's totally up to you, but either way, I'm getting what I want."

"I won't do it!" Her protest was more aggressive this time. The stress and exhaustion she'd been through that night with the fire had removed her instinct for self-preservation. She wouldn't let him do this, not now.

"One last chance," Javi said, coldly, squeezing her painfully where he held her, pressing his thumb into her soft flesh just beneath her shoulder bone.

"No."

"Shame," he tossed the bag into the fire.

The ailing flame reanimated with the newly added fuel, enveloping the leather pouch. It crackled as the gravel stored within caught fire. He let her go, and Fleta immediately got to her feet and grasped a nearby fire poker to rescue the bag. She wouldn't let him win, not this time.

"Oh, by the way," he said, nonchalantly turning his back to her, "if gravel gets too hot, it's ruined. It'll already be ruined even if you get the bag. It won't give him any relief, any high."

He looked back and laughed at her attempt to recover the bag from the flames.

"You heartless prick," she said, turning to face him, tightening her grip on the iron poker. She shouted, louder than she'd ever addressed him before. Her fear of him kept her silent, but not tonight. "You'd force my brother to go through this? You were the one that gave him this addiction!"

"On the contrary," he said, smirking, whilst refusing to match her escalation of energy, "you are the one that forced your brother to go through this. I warned you enough times about letting anyone else know what you were doing to me, and he was suspecting our little relationship."

"We don't have a relationship," she said. "You're a disgusting rapist."

"Don't be like that," he smirked. "You've not said 'no' for years."

She shook with rage as he used her only method of survival against her.

"We get nothing for free in this life," he continued, "Bronson is his own man; he knew what he was doing, don't put his addiction on me."

She still held the poker in her hand, feeling the warm, roughcast iron against her skin. His sneer sealed the deal for her; she knew what she would do. He couldn't hurt her anymore - the elders of the town had decided, they were to be banished. Javi's hold over her would evaporate the moment they crossed the threshold of the Wildlands. He wouldn't ever get an opportunity to kill her brother. All his threats, all her fear, went up in smoke, just like the gravel in the bag behind her.

"I told you, Fleta, my love, I'm going to get what I want, anyway."

As he placed his hand upon her shoulder and increased the pressure on her to force her down to the ground, she lashed out, striking him once with the poker, connecting iron with bone.

The poker was long, black, cast iron, and it had a spear-like tip, with another point two inches long, perpendicular to the first. This secondary point, at a right-angle to the main length of the poker, had embedded itself within Javi's skull, just north of his left ear. His reaction was empty. Fleta wasn't certain whether it was disbelief, or confusion. It was almost as if he didn't feel the pain. His eyes stared into hers, and his expression was blank.

She froze.

Their eyes met; hers exuding all manner of hatred, his of emptiness.

Then, she saw the light return to his eyes, just before all hell broke loose.

He grasped the poker and pulled it out of his skull; small gout of blood erupted from the open wound and settled onto his white shirt at his shoulder, spilling forward onto his chest. He, still disorientated, wrestled the poker from her, but fell backwards, pulling her with him in the struggle. His weakness from the injury was apparent. Gone was the forceful, cold and calculating demon from her worst nightmares; in front of her now was a man shocked by circumstance and struggling for his life; she found it pathetic.

As they both hit the ground, his grasping hand was knocked free from the poker; she used the opportunity to roll away from him, kicking at the wooden table and chairs that lay upturned on the ground from their struggle. She rose to her knees and lifted the poker high.

He punched her in the stomach, drawing all the wind out of her body. She keeled over, dropping the poker as she coughed and gasped. His reactions were slow from the injury, and as he reached for the poker, she flicked it to the side with a sweep of her hand. It clattered along the wooden floorboards, over to the front-door of the house.

He scrambled up, to ensure he was the first to reach it, but she kicked out, hitting his ankle, causing him to hit the ground, falling short of his target. She struggled to regain her breath, but used whatever was remaining within her to leap over his body and grab hold of the iron poker.

She felt comforted by its hard iron surface, as if it belonged with her, as an extension of her being. She rolled over to her back, looking up as Javi got to his feet. He stood over her, then stumbled slightly, before reaching for the poker she gripped in her hands.

In the limited space she had available, she struck out with all her might. The hit landed between the index and middle fingers of his right hand, splitting his hand in two, which was now forked, like a snake's tongue. The errant three fingers flailed around untethered by tendons, and he screamed, stumbling back and falling to the floor, just in front of the hearth.

She climbed up, and quickly scrambled over to him, striking him once more, snapping his wrist. His shock at what was happening to him had long since worn off, and she could tell he now felt every hit. She moved, straddling his body as he screamed from the pain of his hand. Then, she began her revenge.

The following impact smashed against the forearm of his left arm, as he held it up to defend himself, and the one after that was a clean hit to the head. A splatter of blood decorated her face, but she barely noticed. She hadn't realised the power she held. Letting the heavy iron fire poker do most of the work she continued to hit, continued to smash the iron into his skull.

She entered a trance, taking herself away to

her imaginary world.

The meadow of daisies swayed back and forth in the wind; it was a pleasant day, and the warmth from the sun stroked her skin gently. In her imagination, Bronson was there with her this time, holding her hand, and he smiled at her; she smiled back in a way she hadn't for years.

"I'm sorry I couldn't get the gravel for you," she said.

"It's okay Flea," her imagination-conjured Bronson said, "as long as you're with me, I'll be okay."

13

The Hunt

"Why are they after you?" Dawn pleaded with Yuri.

She held him by the arm as she walked in the direction he showed at the riverbank. She could no longer see that face on the opposite side of the river, and Yuri's obtuse deflections did not relieve her anxiety. She found herself regretting lifting him from the river, but quickly scolded herself - he needed help and if she didn't help, he'd be dead. He's blind, injured and alone in unfamiliar territory, she knew she needed to pack away all those feelings to ensure his survival.

They were now several rows of trees deep within the forest on their bank of the river; the sound of the churning rapids had petered out, reintroducing Dawn to the eerie sounds of the forest depths; birds, animal calls, and the whir of the wind as it snaked around the dense trees.

"Please, I must know what I've involved myself in."

"I can't," he said, matter-of-factly, "the best I can do is get to my cache. I have a stick, and some essential supplies to help me navigate these woods. I'll be able to find my way from there, and then you can get back to your friends."

"Then, who are they? Can you tell me that?" She was getting more animated in her pleading, not watching her volume as she probably should be, given that they were being hunted.

After a short silence, Yuri sighed and closed his eyes, "they are, or rather, they were, Devotees of the Sanctuary, like me."

He let the sentence sit for a little too long "They were my colleagues and my brothers… but obviously, that's no longer the case."

Adherents to the teachings of Inauron aren't violent people, they're kind, warm, welcoming. To her, these hunters couldn't both be trying to kill Yuri, and be Devotees of the Sanctuary of Inauron - the juxtaposition of the two roles didn't compute within her mind. Whatever he was keeping back must be damning.

"You expect me to lead you to your cache, but you're not telling me why they're hunting you?" She took a deep breath inward, building her courage. "I should just leave you here."

The cracks and canyons that sat atop his brow deepened, and he sighed.

"Then do what you must," he said quietly, letting go of her arm and stepping ahead.

He fumbled over the brush and uneven ground at his feet; he held his arms out in front of him and waved them back and forth to check for obstacles, almost comically.

She was certain his fumbling was performative, but on the other hand, there was just the slightest chance that by leaving him she was confining him to his fate at the hands of the hunters. This small, minute chance left her with a sickening feeling in the pit of her stomach, and her lips tightened as the shame bubbled up within her breast. She stood, watching this man struggle over the smallest of obstacles, almost fall and injure himself, before she plucked up the courage to overcome her shame.

"I'm sorry," she said, stepping forward and retaking his arm.

He didn't respond but grasped her arm firmly, and shakily exhaled. He had called her bluff, but at that moment, as she retook his arm, hearing his sigh of relief, she believed in his helplessness.

"You're going off-course... here," she led him back to the channel between the rows of trees, and they resumed treading the path as before. "I just feel completely in the dark."

"For all you know, they could chase me for an excellent reason, I understand," his voice wavered a little, "let me at least put you at ease. If they catch up with me, they will kill me. Whatever doubt you have about what I may or may not have done to deserve this treatment, at least you can be comfortable with the fact that this vigilante justice is not justice - this is an unmistakable fact and is even discussed in the Book of Inauron, as I'm sure you're aware."

"The mob delivers no justice; it only inflames the passions of the indignant," she recited.

"You know the teachings well, Dawn," he said. "Even if I were the most heinous person ever to exist, I should still be able to be heard without the threat of death. These ex-brothers will not hear me out; they will not listen to reason; they want one thing from me: my demise."

There was an odd comfort in his dark language; by helping him, she was undoubtedly doing the right thing. Even if Yuri turned out to be the perpetrator and not the victim, she couldn't allow these ex-devotees of the Sanctuary to kill him. She had lived her life until this point treating the Book of Inauron as a series of incredibly important teachings for how one should live their life, and whilst her faith in these teachings had undoubtedly wavered because of their banishment, their wisdom was indisputable.

They walked in relative silence over for what seemed like fifteen minutes, aside from the instructions she occasionally had to give to help him over fallen logs or around bushes. The foliage became ever denser still as they walked; bushes now rose almost to the underside of the tree canopy; enormous, hulking structures that obscured the trunks of the thick trees, darkening their surroundings. Her thoughts moved to this cache; she couldn't imagine how he would identify where this might be. *Can he truly be so familiar with the Wildlands that he can remember exactly where he left something, even without his vision?* Then again, she'd lived her entire life depending on her eyesight and didn't know how her mind would adapt to life without it. *Maybe his vision loss had enhanced some other senses*, she mused.

"What does this cache look like? How are we to know we're going in the right direction?"

"Perhaps you can help with that," he replied. "In this direction, in about five minutes, you should see a tree so large it stands out from those around it. Well, if we push our way through the bushes at ground level, you'll find that the very bottom of the tree's trunk is fully hollow. The hollow is wide enough to open my arms to their longest and barely reach the other end. We'll find what we're looking for there."

She frowned. "This may sound offensive; I don't mean it this way, but how on earth did you find it?"

He chuckled silently, his body vibrating despite the lack of noticeable noise. "No offence taken, I assure you. It's rather simple; things grow here at an alarming rate, it's one of the mysteries of the Wildlands, and despite its current density, that wasn't always the case."

"Oh, so this tree hollow was once obvious?"

"Yes, until I planted the bushes that obscure it," he smiled. "Thirty years is a long time to be out here, and I'm more familiar with these surroundings than you may realise. You'll see what I mean as we approach; look up towards the canopy; the tree we're looking for should punch through it, to the sky."

Her anxiety returned; this time, it was even harder to dismiss. How could he, a blind man, possibly know how the canopy looked? He can't touch or feel the tree's height and certainly can't draw comparisons against the other trees around it; the sensory domain of a blind man exists almost entirely at ground level. Was this a slip-up? Suspicion felt like a binding across her chest, making her breaths shorter. Her eyes darted to their surroundings, convinced that there was something more going on.

Slowly, the anxiety and worry turned to anger, and her lips thinned as she pressed them together. Her fist tightened, and her eyes narrowed. This was a wild-goose chase. She didn't know his game but still felt like an unwilling participant. She breathed through her nose and the muscles on the arm that held him flexed.

"Stop," he said quietly. She obeyed reluctantly. "Do you see it?"

She glanced about near the canopy to find the tree he described, and there it was, punching through the ceiling of foliage to the skies above; near its base lay a bush that obscured most of its trunk, within which Yuri's cache surely lay. She'd hoped for some inaccuracies, something different from his description, perhaps to convince her that he really was blind but was left wanting.

Thirty years without sight, and he could lead her to a random point within these dense woodlands, with a complete visual description? Something didn't add up.

"Please push away some of the bush's branches so that I may enter the hollow," he instructed. Her expression soured at following his instructions, but she did so nonetheless.

As she pulled on one branch, the others moved with it, revealing a large darkened hollow within the enormous tree. No light penetrated beyond the threshold, obscuring completely what may or may not lay within.

"You can pass through now," she offered. Yuri approached, gingerly stepping ahead to feel out any obstacles in his pathway with his toes. He held a hand out before him and waved it back and forth as he moved.

Just as he was moving past her, he quickly grabbed her about the shoulders and pushed her directly into the hollow. It all happened so quickly, she had no time to react before her back and neck clashed with the inner trunk's walls. Before she could cry out in pain, a hand was placed firmly across her mouth cutting any gasps short.

The darkness within the hollow was so perfect that his face in front of hers was reduced to a silvery sliver, the scant light catching just one aspect of his facial contours. Her eyes were wide at his incredulity, and anger boiled within her chest.

She was about to push him off when he lifted a finger to his mouth to show her he needed silence. His head turned to the hollow's entrance, and as the light beneath the canopy caught his expression, she saw his terror. Her ire fell away at once; he was scared, and she surmised he had pushed her inside to keep her from being seen by whoever was outside. Had the hunters found them?

A twig snapped outside the hollow.

Someone was definitely there... approaching.

Yuri slowly removed his hand from her mouth and began moving his arms around them within the hollow near the ground. He was looking for his things, but as his arms moved more frantically, she knew that this hollow was empty.

"Where are your things?" Dawn's voice was barely audible.

"Gone."

She said nothing as he backed away from her; placing his rear against the opposite wall of the hollow, he shook his head.

"I think this was a trap," he replied, "they knew I'd come here."

As her eyes adjusted to the almost complete darkness, she could see his face; head pointed upwards, dejected. Another twig snapped outside the hollow, this one a little closer. Yuri's back slid down the inside wall of the trunk until he sat aground.

Dawn's breathing was unsteady, and her face became reddened. A coldness crept up her spine as she considered that they'd been followed this entire time, lured into a trap, just as Yuri suspected.

The problem with much of the forest around

them is that almost everything was covered in a mossy carpet; the trees, the low branches, the fallen logs, the stones jutting through the earth. It was a surface almost tailor-made for silent movement. She had no idea how close they were or if the sounds they could hear were just that of a deer or some other forest animal.

"What do we do?" Her whisper maintained its low volume, but her speech was shorter, more frantic.

He shrugged, and closed his eyes, resigned to their fate.

She turned her head to listen intently to any sound that made its way to their nook within the tree. The birds had become quiet. The wind whistled as it whipped through the gap in the hollow's entrance. The sounds of the forest had dropped to an unnatural level; it was almost silence. The tree's surface and thick walls deadened much of the noise, but it still felt unnatural to Dawn.

Yuri's hands shook nervously as he placed them over his face, in a lame attempt to hide from the reality of their circumstance.

A voice rang out, but it felt like it was for her alone, within her head; it was deep and gravelly.

"Come out."

"No, I won't do it." She replied aloud. The moment the voice left her lips, Yuri's expression darkened. She knew then that he had not heard this mysterious, terrifying demand.

A shadow moved outside, beyond the bushes.

"Come out," the voice rang out, feeling again like it only existed within her head.

"He's staying right here," she replied aloud once more.

"Please help me," Yuri whimpered.

Her heart melted. He sounded so helpless, so childlike.

"He's not here," she said, "he already left."

"Come out." This was a different voice this time; it sounded more authoritative but was of a higher pitch.

"Come out." Another voice.

"Come." Another.

"Come out." The first voice once more.

Did this mean four of Yuri's ex-brothers were out there or that just four of many spoke to her? Are they even speaking? The sounds seemed to originate within her mind.

She didn't know what to do; she couldn't let them kill him.

"If we come out, do you promise not to hurt us?" She had little hope that this would work, but without a better idea, it was all she had.

"Come out, and we will talk," the second, more authoritative voice spoke slowly.

She was out of options. She knew it, and Yuri knew it too by the haggard expression on his face. She straightened herself up and brushed herself off.

Then, Dawn took a deep breath and stepped out into the blinding forest light.

14

Clearing The Air

Bronson had rushed ahead through the undergrowth, the moment they could hear the river's sound. He threw himself through the foliage to land upon the river bank where Fleta and Kenley said Dawn was waiting, but found no one there. The river flowed loudly as it bent around him, the pebbles and silt crunching at his steps as he paced. His sister and Kenley followed behind him shortly after, surprise written upon their faces when they too realised she was missing.

"You said she might be in danger?" Bronson said to Kenley. "You had a 'vision'?"

"Yeah," Kenley said. "I had hoped what I saw was wrong, and that we'd find her here just sitting by the bank, relaxing."

Then he held up his palms to Bronson, "look,

I know how it sounds... I can't work out if what I saw was happening when I saw it or if it was a premonition or something that had already happened."

"Right..." Bronson replied, tight-lipped. He rubbed an outstretched palm over his head. His hair was too short to tousle in his frustration, but his habit of rubbing his head nevertheless persisted.

"I believe him," Fleta said, "he saw things only I would know."

"Like Javi?" Bronson quipped, "so even Kenley knows what happened, but you've still not told me about it? I'm your twin, Flea. Family means nothing, I guess."

"I will; I've already said I will," Fleta said firmly, "but we need to find Dawn first. Her disappearance is clearly more important."

She walked over to Bronson and grasped his hands. Looking directly into his eyes, she said, "I promise I'll tell you everything once we find her."

She looked scared, and he could feel a slight tremor in her hands as he held them.

Her shattered nerves convinced him she was telling the truth. Resigned, he sighed deeply, "well, we'd better look for her then."

He kept rubbing his hands across his pale, shorn head as he looked around their feet. Darkness inked its way from the water's edge to an area of pebbles near the grass of the forest's edge. It wasn't simply dark; it was wet; he could see now, so he pointed.

"Does your vision say anything about her going in the river? It's all wet here."

The others drew closer to see, Fleta noticed a small scrap of grey fabric nestled between some sharp rocks. She bent and lifted it for the others to inspect.

"She wasn't wearing anything grey," Fleta said, concerned at the find. "She wore a maroon-coloured gown, shaped much like mine."

Kenley looked as white as a sheet; he knew something, Bronson could tell.

"Tell me what you saw in your vision," Bronson commanded. Kenley looked sickened at the prospect.

"I can't," he said.

"Can't or won't," Bronson replied, unwilling to hear any refusal. He needed answers. Fleta kept him in the dark about what happened with their uncle, and now, this idiot hunter-boy was telling them they just needed to trust him. Not today, Bronson decided. He would get his answers.

"I suppose," Kenley thought momentarily, "it's 'won't'."

"Why." It wasn't a question; it was a demand.

"Honestly," he said, looking up at the sky, placing his hands on his hips, "I'm still trying to process what I saw. It was like a bad dream, but when I spoke about it with Fleta she confirmed at least part of what I saw was true… and now I'm afraid everything else in my vision is also true. It was not a good thing to see, Bron."

"You need to tell me," Bronson said, "something you saw in your vision could help us find her."

Kenley pushed his fingers up through his dark brown curls, pushing them tightly to his scalp. "You're right; I know you're right, but that doesn't make it any easier."

He turned and walked in a circle, still keeping his arms around his head.

"The grey fabric was in my vision; I'll say that," he said, hoping Bronson would let it be.

"No," Bronson argued, "tell me what you saw."

It wasn't working, Kenley was closing up and putting up walls around himself. Bronson looked to his sister for help; surely she could also see the need. He spoke to her, but did so in that strange way he did earlier when she was far away from him, speaking as if from within. He had no idea if it would work or, if it was the remnants from his gravel withdrawal playing tricks on his mind, but he had to try.

"Please, Flea, you know we need to hear what

he saw..."

She'd heard him; he knew that much; her eyebrow lifted as he spoke. Kenley however, didn't; he still paced in a circle, wracking his brain, attempting to make sense of what he saw, without a hint of recognition that Bronson had just spoken.

"How are you doing this?" Fleta replied aloud.

"I don't know," Bronson replied, honestly. "Perhaps I'll tell you when you tell me about Javi."

At that, she looked to the ground, but Bronson wasn't sure if it was shame or annoyance. In truth, he wasn't even sure he could explain how it worked to his sister. This ability seemed so innate, so obvious; as automatic as breathing or operating his arms or legs. It didn't *feel* alien to him, but he knew it was - and that odd juxtaposition made the hairs on his arms rise.

It was that realisation that made him look to Kenley more sympathetically. Was he going through something similar? Was this prophetic vision that he purported to have in some way connected to Bronson's own ability to communicate with his sister this way?

"Kenley," Bronson said, altering his tone to a more friendly one, "I can talk to people through their minds."

Kenley stopped and looked at him, frowning.

"See, that look, right there," Bronson said, pointing at Kenley's puzzled visage. "That is the look I gave you when you first mentioned your vision, but I think we can acknowledge that there's something about this place that's fucking with us."

Kenley said nothing, just stared back at him, blankly.

"Can you hear this?" Bronson spoke to Kenley's mind, just like he did with his sister.

His eyes widened, and Bronson took that as an acknowledgement.

"How are you doing that? Is this how you spoke to Fleta to find us?" Kenley said, with a single eyebrow lifted.

"I don't know, and yes."

Kenley frowned and dipped his eyes to the ground.

"All I'm saying is," Bronson continued, "is that whatever is happening to us, out here, is weird and strange and unnatural. This vision you had is probably the same; it's not your fault."

Kenley sat upon the mossy ground, leaning his back against a tree. He looked to the sky and then rubbed his hands down his face, pausing when each hand hid each half of his face to take a deep breath. Bronson and Fleta joined him on the ground, Bronson knew that if he was to get the information he wanted, then he had to make

Kenley feel at ease.

"I saw a lot of things, fast," he started, "almost as if I were observing them from above, like a bird; some flashes were more detailed than others."

He seemed to have accepted his fate as this storyteller as much as it pained him. A tear ran down his cheek, but he'd already started now, Bronson could see his determination to finish.

"I saw your uncle, but I'll let Fleta tell you all about that when she's ready."

Fleta gave Kenley a tight smile, acknowledging his gratitude.

"I saw Lawson being tortured by some people who looked like they were made of stone." He took a breath. "I saw Addison running with Corin in his arms; she looked dead, like really dead, like the life had been sucked right out of her. I saw some grey-robed men locking everyone in the Grove into the town hall, then they set it on fire.

He gulped and breathed loudly in and out through his nose, "and I saw Dawn with some of these grey-robed men spread out on the ground in front of her."

Bronson gasped involuntarily. He felt so strongly for Dawn that he couldn't bare the thought of her in danger, but he needed to know.

"What do you mean 'spread out'?"

"I mean dead," Kenley said, returning his eyes

to the pebbles at his feet. "Dawn was covered in blood, and it looked like she'd done it... like, she had killed them."

Fleta's nervous tremor became more pronounced.

"What do you mean?" Bronson asked as he grasped his sister's hand to comfort her. "Dawn couldn't hurt anyone; she's tiny."

"This is why I struggled to tell you, it makes little sense to me, none of it does." Kenley protested.

"How do we know *any* of it is true?"

"I didn't, or don't, want any of it to be true," he said. "But what I saw of Fleta is true; she confirmed it. It happened. Which means there's a chance everything else happened too... or will happen... or is happening right now."

His mind was brought back to his dear uncle Javi whose fate was still undetermined in his mind - he didn't want to believe Fleta's declaration of his death, it was too out of character for Fleta. As he thought about it some more, slaying four grey-robed men was out of character for Dawn, too. Were they all acting differently? What had happened to them out here.

If he chose not to believe that Fleta was capable of murder, then, in this roundabout way, he knew he couldn't believe anything of Kenley's vision, either. Therefore, it made him realise, that confirmation of one story will validate all the others. He needed to know what happened between Javi and his sister.

He looked to Fleta, but she shied away from his gaze.

"Tell me what happened," he said quietly. "I need to understand this whole thing."

He kept his eyes on his sister, and she defiantly looked away. Both were in this stalemate, and neither would waver.

"Let's try to find Dawn," Kenley said, attempting clumsily to break the tension, but the siblings were resolute.

"Fleta," Bronson said, "tell me what happened."

"Guys, she's in danger," Kenley protested.

"Tell me," Bronson said, raising his voice, "what are you hiding?"

Fleta broke down into sobs but still said nothing.

"Bron, stop," Kenley shouted.

"You stay the fuck out of this," Bronson said, pointing directly at him, gripped by anger. Kenley recoiled.

Bronson couldn't even form a picture of what *might* have happened in his mind; it was just one big unknown. His gentle but withdrawn sister is hiding something from him. She shouldn't ever have to hide anything from him; they used to tell each other everything; they used to know everything that went on in each other's heads. They used to be open books to each other. This refusal to open up represented how much their relationship as twins had eroded in recent years.

Bronson knew he couldn't let up, he couldn't spare her feelings... this was supremely important, not just because it concerned the fate of a dear uncle - one of the people he loved most in this world - but because knowing what happened would validate Kenley's vision. Then they could use it to find Dawn.

"She doesn't want to tell you, yet," Kenley said, Bronson balled his hand up into a fist and stared Kenley down.

"I said, stay the fuck out of it."

"Let it go," Kenley spat.

Bronson stood.

Kenley joined him.

They stared at each other, each daring the other to make the first move. Kenley was around half a foot shorter than him and a good deal less muscular, so he knew he'd find it no trouble to overpower the boy.

"Stop it, both of you," Fleta cried out; her eyes were red and tear-filled. "You want to know what happened to your beloved uncle? Your best friend?"

Bronson relaxed his clenched grip, then looked intently at his ailing sister.

"Well, I killed him..." she shouted, "I beat him to death until the ground under him was covered in his brains."

She took a deep breath, and Bronson's blood ran cold. His extremities seemed to drain of life immediately and he collapsed back down to the ground in front of her. Her voice was hoarse, and he couldn't remember the last time he'd heard his sister at this volume; the timid, quiet girl was gone.

"And you know why I did it? Do you know why, Bron?" she said, venom in her voice, "I did it to protect you. Everything I've ever done in this life is to protect you! That's why I said nothing about him over the years, about everything I've had to put up with, because I knew that deep down I had to do it, or else he'd kill everyone I've ever loved, starting with you, brother."

Bronson couldn't find the words; he stammered fumbling over every letter of his nonsensical response. It couldn't be true, could it? His uncle was kind and wouldn't ever hurt him; what could she possibly be protecting him from?

Finally, after much stuttering, "what do you mean, protect me?"

"Yeah, that's right, Bron," she said.

"From what?" Bronson said. "What were you protecting me from? Javi wouldn't kill anyone, that's madness."

"Don't make me say it, Bron," Fleta said.

"What did Javi do?"

She gulped, took a deep breath, closing her eyes as she prepared herself. As her eyelids shuttered, a single glassy tear ran down her cheek. Whatever she wasn't telling him clearly pained her incredibly. He knew he had to be compassionate, but this whole situation just didn't feel real. These people he knew and loved had somehow been granted entirely new personalities... either that, or Bronson was just too stupid to see them clearly.

"He raped me and beat me nearly every single day for the last ten years..." she said. Bronson's mouth fell open and his eyes widened. "...and I couldn't say anything because if I did, he promised to kill you."

When did the tears start flowing? He had no recollection. And when did his wailing begin?

Before he knew it, his arms were wrapped tightly around his sister, pulling her in as close as he could muster as she wailed along with him.

His uncle had done a stellar job at indoctrinating him from a young age and keeping all knowledge of his terror away from him. All this time, he'd believed his uncle when he explained why Fleta was so miserable. He'd believed the excuses he'd been given.

Even with all that, there was no doubt in his mind that what Fleta was telling him was true. Everything he knew about his sister supported her version of events; she was unwavering in her love for her family, she would do anything to protect him and their parents, even endure years of unimaginable torment.

"I'm sorry," he said between sobs, "you should never have had to do that."

Bronson had failed as a brother. It was his role to protect her, but he'd been more interested in getting high and having fun with her abuser. Bile rose in his throat, burning him from the inside. He would fix it. He had to. He vowed then to spend his life making it up to her; she would now be his single purpose for living. He would fix this by giving his entire life to her, forever.

15

Appropriate Justice

As she left the safe confines of the tree's hollow, Dawn's eyes took a moment to adjust to the bright light piercing the canopy above her. Dim though the surrounding light was, the contrast between the darkness of the hollow and the surrounding woodland was enough to take her eyes time to adjust. As her focus on the scene grew sharper, she saw three dark-robed figures standing near the path.

"Ah, our wayward little friend," the first one said. She recognised this as the more authoritative voice that spoke to her whilst within the hollow. The other two stood silently, eyes fixated upon her.

The trunk of the tree was a few steps up a rise from the path, and so she gingerly stepped down to the area between the trees she'd been only moments earlier.

The silence that followed was cut with tension.

The leader of this group of ex-devotees stared at her to encourage a response, but the mixture of her fear and resolve prevented her from returning anything but a matched glare. They both played this battle of silence, willing each other to be the first to break.

He walked over to a moss-covered log near the path and took a seat, never taking his eyes from hers before finally gesturing to a large flat rock on the opposite side.

"I think I'll stay right here," Dawn replied.

The leader's eyes flicked briefly to behind her left shoulder, and she felt an enormous hand grasp her by the arm. She turned to look at whatever had grabbed her; it was the same face she had seen in the trees across the river that had started this ill-fated excursion. His face was almost covered with a mass of dark grey and black hair; the hairline of his facial hair ended far closer to his eyes than she'd ever known in a man, and he had deep-set piercing blue eyes. She recalled that these were the same eyes that had scared her into helping Brother Yuri. She froze at the sight of him and as a result; he could pull her easily to the stone where the leader of the group waited. The bear-man exerted pressure upon her shoulders, and she sat reluctantly upon the stone, he then seemed to disappear into the brush behind her like a phantom, the moment his job was done.

"I am Brother Alex," the man said, with an air of authority. He was middle-aged, clean shaven, with light brown hair sat neatly upon his scalp. He didn't look threatening; but he didn't have to, since he was travelling with such an enormous, ursine companion. "This pair behind me are Brother Teus and Brother Magalan... and the large-looking fellow that brought you to your seat is Brother Cillian."

He paused, eyes closing briefly as he took a deep breath.

Brother Teus was a gaunt, bald, dark-skinned man that found it very difficult to meet Dawn's gaze. Magalan on the other hand was a tall, lithe, pale, and burned his stare into her like he was trying to see into her very soul. They all unnerved her in equal part. All three wore grey robes matching Brother Yuri, with a gold embroidered tree symbol upon the breast.

"Why are you chasing Brother Yuri?" she blurted.

A sinister grin grew across his face.

"Why are you so keen to stand in the way of righteous justice?"

He leaned back a little, lifting a leg to cross over his other before settling back forward. His dark colourless eyes continued to stare at her from just above his long interlocked fingers. He was middle-aged; his hair had not yet greyed though it had receded at the edges of his scalp.

"This doesn't look like any justice I've heard of. It's certainly not Inauron's justice," she scoffed.

Dawn was very familiar with the teachings of Inauron. A group of Brothers harassing an ailing blind man through the woods wasn't even the remotest possibility in the teachings, in-fact there were many teachings specifically against such action.

"Ah, we've got ourselves a little scholar," Alex smiled as he turned to his companions. "a girl after my own heart, what are the chances?"

He continued, "so, what are you after? Are you attempting to insert yourself into this proceeding of justice?"

"I obviously can't get in your way if you want to do this," she started, "but at least tell me why and give me a chance to convince you to spare him."

Brother Alex smoothed at his chin whilst he considered his options.

Dawn bore no love for Brother Yuri; she was almost certain he was deceptive and cunning, but she believed that these Brothers, his former companions, were threatening his life. Whatever he had done, he deserved to be treated with the respect due a lifelong servant of Inauron. She couldn't allow him to be slaughtered in the woods. If his crime was so great he should stand trial and be convicted and sentenced accordingly.

Brother Alex grumbled, "just so we're clear, you're not speaking to a bunch of uneducated brutes, I am fully certified as a Righteous Justiciar of the Brothers of Inauron, a companion sect of the Church of Inauron, and as a result, my word *is* the law when it comes to matters under the purview of the Brothers."

Dawn was suspicious; she'd never heard of these 'Brothers of Inauron' and knew of no separate sects of the Church of Inauron. She had mistakenly assumed that when Brother Yuri told her who he was, he was simply part of the monastic tradition within the central Church. She'd studied this as part of her religious education.

"My decision alone allows me to distinguish between cases and try them with or without a sitting jury. The Brothers of Inauron aren't part of the populace of Gilgannon and although we look it, we're not your standard devotees of the Church. We have our own laws and our own ways of meting out justice," Brother Alex said. "That being said, you've piqued my curiosity, so I will allow you to speak. Let me first understand to whom we address... please indulge me in a hypothetical scenario. Before I allow you to plea for Brother Yuri's life, I want to know where you stand on justice as a whole."

She nodded her assent; curious as to what he spoke of. He was convincing, but Brother Alex here spoke deeply about something that she'd never heard of which raised her guard. Who were the Brothers of Inauron?

"Let's say a standard punishment for thievery is a single lash on the accused's back in the village square," he started, staring intently at her as he spoke. "If a man steals some bread, what should be his punishment?"

She frowned, "a single lash in the village square?"

He nodded. "How about if this bread was freely given to others by a baker with an endless supply of bread, what then? Does the act of theft rely on the scarcity of the stolen merchandise?"

"The punishment should fit the crime. Here, there doesn't seem to be a crime."

She thought momentarily, "if the man took the bread without asking, but the baker was giving it away regardless, then perhaps the man should be let off with a warning."

"Interesting response."

Brother Alex thought for a moment longer.

"Let's take this hypothetical a little deeper,

shall we?" he asked. She nodded. "What if the bread was given to a pauper on the brink of starvation to save their life, and the man stole this bread resulting in the poor pauper's untimely death? Standard punishment? More severe? Less severe?"

"The man indirectly caused the death of another, so it should be more severe, but shouldn't be treated as if the man caused the death directly."

"I see we are of one mind," he smirked.

Dawn suddenly felt as though she was being led into a trap that had yet to spring. Her heart began beating faster, and her cheeks flushed. What was his game?

Brother Alex continued, "in all three scenarios the man's intent and action are identical, but what's changed is the context. I'm glad we agree that context is important, because in our case, the crime itself will seem like nothing more than an unfortunate accident."

"If you wish to convince me of appropriate justice," he said, opening his arms to convey sincerity, "then allow me to convince you of my position, as well. I'm certain we can strike an accord."

She was feeling ensnared in a battle of wits and so she tightened her lips in determination. She knew she couldn't run; she knew she couldn't fight; it was just her resolve against the Brothers'.

"The crime in question feels like nothing more than property damage, which I'm sure you'll agree does not warrant death, so I'll do what I can to explain the context," he said. "Feel free to disagree, but based on your answers to my hypotheticals, I'm certain you won't."

"We'll see about that," she said, her defiance showing. "I can't imagine a circumstance where property damage would lead to death without trial."

He took a deep breath and started, "The damaged property was important to the Church."

"It should still be treated as an accident," she rebutted.

"It was a ward; an artifact of protection, to keep others safe."

"Again, still an accident," she said, but before he could continue she added, "unless something happened as a result, of course."

"As a result," he expertly used her phrasing against her to continue, smirking as he did, "a deadly poison was released into a town centre."

She stayed silent this time; she didn't feel like she had enough information about this. Rapidly, this academic discussion made her feel out of her depth. Was this the snare she suspected closing around her? She held the skirt of her wool gown in her fist, as she tried her best to find reason in his words.

"This poison affected every member of this town and indirectly caused significant casualties."

His voice became more direct, more aggressive.

His volume increased a little, "a poison for which there is no known cure."

Louder, "a poison that until neutralised at its source will continue to seep out into the world."

"Those poisoned have no option but death," he said, now pointing at her and gritting his teeth. "So to then should the person who created this disaster."

She gulped.

After a pause that seemed to last an eternity, Brother Alex sat back, smiled softly and spoke in a calmer tone. "What say you then, my little wayward friend, should the accused be executed?"

Her heart was telling her to save Brother Yuri, but if what Brother Alex was saying was true, then she could do nothing more for him.

He should die.

She had no inkling what the Brothers of Inauron code of justice would say, but even in the Church, she knew that such a disaster would inevitably end in execution, regardless of whether she agreed with that outcome.

She trembled.

"I..." she started; her mind scrambled for a way out, desperate to find a route to saving his life, but all her avenues were closing around her.

"I think," she said, her heart pounded in her chest, "if what you're saying is all true, then I'm not sure what I can do."

Brother Alex's sweet smile turned into a sneer.

"I should tell you," he grinned, "before we address this even further... that Brother Yuri has done nothing wrong."

She grimaced, confused.

Was this a game to him?

What is he trying to do?

"Brother Yuri is, in-fact, not why we're here."

The trap had sprung, Brother Alex knew it, but Dawn hadn't yet grasped what was happening; every further word confused her even more.

"We're here for you," his eyes levelled at her. Gone was the mock joviality he'd shown throughout their debate.

"It is you, Dawn and friends, who we are here to pass sentence on."

Her blood turned to ice. Her breathing became erratic. A tremble settled upon her extremities,

"No," she whispered, "we've done nothing of the sort."

"The 'ward' I mentioned, is the precious tree at the centre of your Sanctuary, which, as you know, has been summarily destroyed by you and your ilk."

Disbelief was etched into her expression; her eyebrows pushed to the sky, her mouth fell open.

"Everyone you know and love is dead," he said. Her stomach churned. "Poisoned by your hand."

"It wasn't me," Dawn pleaded as she stood. "I didn't start the fire."

"Who did is irrelevant, it was one of either you or your nine friends, all of which will be hunted and killed."

She had no words. A ringing began in her ears, drowning out the ambient sounds of the forest, and dampening any further words he said.

"I'm glad you agree with my idea of appropriate justice," he said, but her mind was elsewhere, "it will make it so much easier to round up your friends with an ally like you."

"I won't help you," Dawn protested, breath short.

"You mean, you now miraculously disagree with this justice?" He drew a sinister grin, then addressing his companions he continued, "who would have thought? She wants to save everyone, even those due to be executed. How quickly the opinion of justice has changed!"

"I won't help you kill my friends," she cried.

"I have it on good authority that three of your friends are seeking you out as we speak!"

A gasp caught in her throat.

Brother Alex's eyes turned a milky white as he spoke directly into her mind like he did when she was within the hollow, "hmmm.... Kenley Coyde, Fleta Timber and her twin brother Bronson."

The Brothers of Inauron had caught her in their trap. There was nothing she could do; she'd been ingeniously led here, and the snare was closing around her, suffocating her thoughts. Brother Alex was a cunning villain who had willingly got her to consent to her own demise.

She knew she had to die.

If everything he said was accurate, and the fire had caused the death of everyone from Penny Grove, then she had no option. If she was to remain faithful to the Church and all it represents, she'd willingly walk to the gallows...

...but she wouldn't let them take her friends.

She thought of innocent and foolish Kenley

unwittingly tracking her and leading the others into an ambush. She thought of Fleta, her beautiful broken friend, who'd been at her side for as long as she could remember. And she thought of her childhood sweetheart Bronson, who she had spurned for Addison, but never stopped loving. They didn't deserve any of this. The ice in her veins thawed... then boiled. She couldn't let these Brothers take them.

She stood, turned to look for a way out, and saw the ursine Brother Cillian stood beside her, his mountainous form blocking her escape. Her ire rose, and she clenched her fist, trying her best to conceal her rage.

"You're not leaving," Alex said calmly, infuriating her even more.

She gritted her teeth and could feel the colour returning to her face. She breathed loudly out of her nose like a steam boiler about to blow. Her anger reached a fever pitch, and she lashed out.

Her hand struck Brother Cillian, a man nearly twice her height and at least three times her weight. She barely felt the impact in her hand or arm, it was as if she had thrown her fist through a cloud, but Cillian's head began to turn with the blow. Dawn could clearly hear the crunch and grind of the bones of his spine fracturing and being destroyed. Almost as if in slow-motion, she saw his body take to the air then fall to the ground nearby, his face pointing in the wrong direction to his body.

"She's awakened!" Brother Alex screamed as Teus and Magalan leapt into action.

"Abomination!" Teus yelled as he tried to grasp one of her arms, Magalan the other.

She shook herself free with surprising ease and bore her fingernails in a blow to Brother Teus' face. Her fingers drew lines in his flesh as if she was running them through sand, four enormous rivulets tore down his visage, spilling his blood out like a trickling fountain from each of the wounds. His resultant scream coated her in his blood as he flailed about.

She turned to Brother Magalan and punched with such force that she could see the muscles and tendons around his throat rupture as it bent backwards; the skin split, and his head became almost free entirely of his neck and shoulders. Despite the separation, his mouth continued to scream soundlessly; his eyes remained open as he fell to the ground. Blood began to gout from his open neck, staining the grasses and low-lying plants.

In her rage, she faced Brother Alex, who backed up from her in terror. She leapt across the path to him and pounded upon his head and face as he screamed, turning his face into something no longer human, with little resemblance to the being he once was. Her mind was singularly focused on her task, and she bore no thoughts or consideration for her actions. Her rage was all-consuming.

She stood and surveyed the devastation before her. Four bodies, impossibly destroyed. Brother Teus' screaming from his facial wounds petered out, and he lost consciousness from the blood loss. She couldn't stop her rage; it was overtaking her, boiling out of every orifice. She felt hot and overwhelmed, with a deep intoxication at her power.

She did this.

And she liked it.

So drunk with rage was she, that she didn't hear Brother Yuri emerge from the hollow within the tree. She didn't hear him pick up a fist-sized rock from the ground. She didn't hear the swing of his arm.

The sweet void of darkness enveloped her.

16

Hot and Bloody Trail

Jessil opened the dilapidated door to his shed, carrying over his shoulder the slain carcass of a deer. The door struggled to stay open long enough for him to get through.

"Get the door, boy," he told his son, Kenley, who was only eight years old. Kenley duly rushed ahead and pulled the door open from inside, allowing his father to walk in with the carcass. A hoof grazed his scalp as his father turned into the dimly lit wooden shed.

The dark and musty old-wood interior deadened the dull thud of Jessil dropping the deer onto the long table set up along the room's width. Dust motes escaped from their hiding places throughout the structure, giving the interior an almost magical quality, as each speck danced in the sparse sunlight through the single window behind the table.

It was a fresh kill and one of the only times Kenley could remember when his father had willingly attempted to connect with his son and bring him into his trade.

Kenley loved the idea of hunting, of hiding in the brush and taking down deer or even smaller game. He loved tracking and felt at home in the woods, but, as with every trade, a side of it existed that was far less palatable. The timber traders within the town, who made up the most of all external trade, were often passionate about managing the timber; chopping, sizing and preparing for sale, but many hated the required accounting that went along with it. This is why his friend Addison's family, the Ruthands, became leaders in accounting within the town. Hunting was no different, though the unpalatable thing for Kenley wasn't numbers; it was the inevitable butchery.

His father attempted to include him in the meat and hide preparation but not in the part that Kenley actually enjoyed, which irked him. Even as an eight-year-old, Kenley could appreciate the unfairness of his father's efforts. He wanted to go hunting with his father and experience the camaraderie and teamwork required to take down big game. Still, the only olive branch his father would offer was for his son to stand by as Jessil butchered the creature in front of him.

First, his father took a thin knife and made a cut within each of the animal's hind legs, then pushed a long cylinder of wood similar to a sweeping brush handle through the gaps in the flesh he made, bridging between the legs.

"Here, help me with this," Jessil had instructed as he lifted the body. "Take the hook on the frame over there, and place it under the wooden brace here."

Kenley could barely reach the hook at the top of a tall frame of wood, partly because of his height but also because the shed's small size didn't support two people manoeuvring about within. The animal would hang upside down, face almost touching the ground, freely able to sway and be turned as necessary during the skinning and butchering.

His father walked around the frame to the back, where a chain ran to the ground. He grasped and pulled downwards, lifting the carcass higher.

"Get the bucket and place it under the head," his father said.

As he did so, his father wrapped the chain around a small hook at the bottom to keep it in place. Then with a quick movement and with no warning, he slit the deer's throat. Thick blood that looked black in the low light began flowing from the wound into the bucket. The tapping of the inconsistent flow onto the metallic surface of the bucket was melodic, but once the bucket filled beyond an inch of depth, the noise became a soft slapping of wetness that turned his stomach.

He remembered the smell more than anything about that afternoon; as his father cut into the meat, he recalled a wet, cold aroma with metallic notes. The scent had stuck with him even now after so many years. He could place it at a moment's notice. It had baggage; it smelled of gore, but more than anything, he associated it with his father's absence, his father's unwillingness to understand why Kenley despised it. It symbolised their growing distance and Jessil's attitude towards parenting.

Kenley had smelt nothing like it before, and hadn't since.

Until now.

He stared in horror at the corpses of the four men in silence, a silence that broke only as he heard Fleta vomiting into the bushes behind them.

"It's just like my vision," were the only words he could muster.

"Where was Dawn in your vision," Bronson asked him as he stood behind, rubbing his sister's back as she brought up more of the scant provisions they were using to sustain themselves in their exile.

Kenley walked over to where Dawn stood in his vision; on the ground below him was a body barely recognisable as human; everything above the neck was pulverised.

"Here," he said slowly. "She had a look in her eyes that made me realise that this was her work."

"But you didn't see it happen in your vision, just her standing there?"

"Just standing here, yes."

"Well, maybe she didn't do this?"

"I'd love to believe that," he looked up at Bronson as he spoke. "I can't explain it, but I know it was her."

Bronson looked pained, worried. He hadn't left his sister's side since her revelation by the river, and Kenley could see Bronson's emotional state begin to fray. He'd just found out about his sister's horrifying history with their uncle, and now had to contend with the girl he'd been in love with since they were children horrifically mutilating these people, whoever they were. Kenley looked at him with sympathy but couldn't give him any respite; his vision was brief and showed little beyond what they saw spread out in front of them.

Fleta coughed as she struggled to bring up

anything else, then she stood, wiping at her mouth. "You talked to me, Bron."

Bronson looked at her and frowned, not understanding what she meant.

"You were miles away from us in this forest, but somehow you talked to me. You could follow the sound of my voice to figure out where we were," she placed the back of her hand at her mouth as if staving off the urge to throw up once more, then continued, "you did it again a few minutes ago by the river, to Kenley."

Bronson closed his eyes, knowing what must be done, "I don't understand it, though; it just happened."

"Use it to talk to Dawn; find her."

"I don't know how it works," he said, throwing his arms up. "I don't even know whether it only lets me talk to you because we're twins and Kenley because I could see him in front of me."

Kenley could see the anxiety on his face; he knew he had an ability that allowed him to find Dawn but didn't want to use it, because doing so would force him to speak not with the Dawn his childhood crush, but with Dawn the violent monster... and that was something he wasn't yet ready to believe.

Something strange was happening to them in this forest; they were developing abilities that seemed at odds with nature. Kenley had visions of the past and future, Bronson could speak to someone regardless of distance, and Dawn had somehow committed this atrocity. He didn't *know* Dawn had done this, of course, but the feeling the scene gave him was undeniable. He recalled that look in her eyes, stood there, covered with their blood... So far, his vision had shown him events that had happened or were about to happen; he had no reason to doubt what he saw.

"I don't know how the vision worked, either," Kenley said, "I know how you feel."

"But you've got to try," Fleta protested.

She stepped over the bodies, following the small game trail that led through the trees, "let's just walk over here, away from all of this."

Bronson rubbed at his face, resigned to his fate, and followed his sister.

They approached a part of the trail with some large rocks, and Fleta sat upon one of them.

"Give it a go," she instructed her brother.

Bronson sat upon a stone, closed his eyes and took a deep breath.

Kenley waited for something to happen.

He shared an anxious glance with Fleta, as they waited with bated breath.

Kenley turned away from the devastation

a little down the path, but he couldn't shake the smell. His mouth was involuntarily downturned as he tried not to breathe through his nose.

After what seemed to be an eternity, Bronson threw his arms up, then stood and growled at the sky.

"I don't know how this works," he screamed, and paced back and forth. "I just got silence, and I don't know if that's because I can't do it, or that I can do it, but not to Dawn, or I can do it, but Dawn's not able to answer me, or something completely different and unrelated. How can I know?"

He rubbed at his temples.

Kenley stood.

"I'll try to track her; stay here as I go back to..." he gestured toward the bodies, "... over there, and see if I can find her trail."

Fleta walked over to comfort her brother, sitting him back down upon the rock and placing an arm around him.

When he returned to the massacre - if he could call it that - he stood exactly where he saw Dawn in his vision. Lots of the typical signs of passage would be concealed by the welts in the dirt and broken twigs caused by whatever had occurred here. It would be a trying task to sort the real clues of passage from those attributed to the battle. He needed to step backwards and assess a larger area around the outside of the site; he needed to find something that he was more certain happened after the fight.

He walked backwards, then around slowly, arcing around the large tree behind where the fight had occurred. He stepped gingerly over moss-ridden stones and logs, careful not to damage or alter the scene. He spied a hollow within the giant tree's trunk as he approached. Curiosity piqued his interest, and he pushed through the bushes at the entrance that partially concealed it.

Pinned to the opposite face of the hollow with a slim knife was a piece of parchment.

He couldn't make out what was on it in the darkness, so he eased out the knife, and stepped back into the light, with the parchment in his hands. On it was scratched a crude map, the tree was shown in the bottom right, and an arrow snaked around some smaller pictures until it eventually ended at a tent and fire at the top left. En route to this campsite, the line dipped around a fallen log suspended above a path, then what looked to depict a clearing with a large rock at its centre, then a gnarled ancient tree.

Who had left this for them?

Confused, he turned it over and saw words upon its back.

"We have Dawn. Find us."

His heart sank; she had been captured.

17

The Fire Inside

Bronson's heart leapt as he read the parchment that Kenley had found; she was alive. They needed to find her; they needed to get her back. He needed it.

He took the lead, holding the parchment aloft as they followed the barely visible game trail set into the channel between rows of trees.

It took some time to decide on which direction they needed to walk in. They each took turns standing at various points in the small space between the trees and holding the parchment up to check the angle that the hollow tree was drawn at.

Eventually they settled on a direction and started pushing forward. Bronson powered through the undergrowth, distracting himself from all that he'd experienced over the last few hours with swift and decisive action.

Right under his nose, his uncle, the person who he regarded as his best friend, was destroying his sister in every way, without his knowledge. How could he have missed the signs? It was driving him insane that he didn't know. As his mind wandered on the journey to the campsite, he recalled a decade of events and pored over them to figure out what he'd missed and how he could have committed such a tremendous error in judgement. His sister, who, shortly after Javi arrived at Penny Grove, had morphed inexplicably from a warm, funny, and upbeat companion to being a cold, miserable wretch. Knowing the reason why, made him sick. He had naively believed Javi's lies about her mood as something all women go through. He'd trusted his uncle. He was desperate to find something concrete that he'd missed or misread. He needed a reason to hate himself for allowing this to go on under his nose. It wasn't his pain or story, but that didn't take away any of the feelings of responsibility. He had failed as a brother.

And now, on top of this horrific bombshell, he had to contend with the fact that Dawn, the only person he'd ever truly loved, might be some kind of monster. What in Inauron's grace was happening to them?

They turned a corner, and Bronson slid to

a halt. Above them was a large fallen tree that rested atop two verges either side of the path, creating a tunnel with an enormous, rotten log roof.

"This is the first landmark," Kenley said, breaking the group's quiet. "At least we know we're going in the right direction now."

Bronson ducked beneath the log that rested across the path at just below his height. Fleta and Kenley could just step beneath it without ducking.

They didn't stop moving, and continued to the next landmark.

Bronson felt something building within him as he moved; his temperature seemed to fluctuate irrespective of the movements of the surrounding breeze, and his head seemed to lose mass, giving him an airy, spaced-out feeling. His stomach was in knots, and his vision seemed to blur with his temperature. He shook the feeling off, now wasn't the time to return to the sickness he'd felt that morning.

They hadn't yet considered what they would do when they got this mysterious campsite. Planning, right now, seemed like wasted time when Dawn life could be in peril. He just knew they had to get there as soon as possible. In the back of his mind, he considered what were they walking into. He was certain it was a trap, or an ambush, else why would these kidnappers have given them directions to rescue their friend.

He pictured his uncle out of instinct, as he usually did when feeling uncertain about something; his uncle had spent so many years as a confidant and mentor that he'd thought about him without considering what he now knew. Javi's face was distorted in his minds-eye; his visage was twisted into a depiction of evil, with red glowing pupils and a grin that stretched almost from ear to ear.

"You never suspected a thing," this abominable Javi barked at him, and with that, Bronson fell to the ground, collapsing under the weight of his burdens. All that had occurred could no longer be subdued from surfacing and affecting him. He tried to put on a brave face for the sake of his sister, but the floor caught up to him far quicker than he was expecting.

Fleta was at his side immediately. Kenley held him by one arm, his sister by the other as they tried to lift him from the ground.

"Bron, are you okay?"

"No," he whispered almost involuntarily before rising to a shout, "you're not supposed to comfort me; I need to comfort you."

Fleta tightened her jaw.

"How did I miss what he was doing to you?" Bronson cried, tears running down his face. "How didn't I see?"

Fleta refused to get taken in by his emotion, "this is not on you, Bron. He was manipulative, evil and cunning. I saw how he was with people - you cannot blame yourself."

Kenley and Fleta relaxed their grip as they leaned her brother against a tree alongside the path.

"Why didn't you tell me?" Bronson's voice had retreated almost to a whimper.

"Fear," she said flatly. "I was young; didn't understand what he was doing at first. When I did, I'd unfortunately learned the depths of his evil. I didn't want any of that for you."

"You still should have said something..." he whispered.

"If I even thought about telling anyone, he would show me exactly what he'd do in retaliation," she said, soothing him. "I was scared, Bron. I've never been more scared."

"I would have endured anything to see you safe; I would have given everything if you'd just told me."

"I know." She took a deep breath. "And that's exactly why I didn't."

He looked at her, trying to divine her meaning.

"In keeping quiet, I had to endure something painful, but in the end... I was alive, you were alive, and our parents were alive. If I'd told anyone, Javi would have killed you all; I absolutely believe he was capable of it. I had to make a snap decision; do something that would cause me to have my entire family murdered, or do nothing and keep them safe."

His cry became louder, "but it's my job to protect you. I should have done my job."

"It was never your job," she said firmly, holding his head in her hands. "This isn't your responsibility."

"Stop comforting me," he snapped. "I'm supposed to be comforting you."

Fleta's pained expression told him all he needed to know, that he'd failed at being a brother. He felt worthless.

"Why does this hurt so much?" he cried. His tears wet his cheeks, and he wiped at his running nose with his sleeve.

"I've been dealing with this pain for ten years, Bron." Her jaw was set, and her eyes lowered at him. "What you're feeling now is what I felt every single day. This feeling of not knowing what to do... not understanding what was happening, or why it all happened to you... this has been my life for what seems like forever."

"Do you know when I stopped feeling like that?" She continued without waiting for a response; her voice was quiet but firm, "it was the moment Councillor Adair announced our exile.

Suddenly the life that I was protecting, the safety of my brother and family, mattered no more, like the rug was pulled from under it. It made me realise that life within Penny Grove, trying to maintain everyone's safety and the status quo of being a doting lumberer's daughter, just didn't matter. I was never going to have a life there; I was never going to grow old there, get married, or have children... This fiction I'd created in my mind, the life I'd been predicting, the very thing that got me through the worst of what happened to me, would never come to pass; it was false, a lie."

He looked up at her, tears welled up in her own eyes as she recounted her pain.

"That's why I killed the cunt," she said, venom in her voice. "I killed him because none of it mattered anymore."

It hurt him so much to hear his sister talk this way. She mattered to him; she was important to him. He hadn't shown her love for years, and he wished he had never bought into Javi's stories about her.

"Get up," she told him.

He couldn't. His body didn't want to comply with his wishes; it was rooted to the ground giving him no authority over it.

She stood, brushed herself off, and gently pushed Kenley aside to give them space.

"Get up," she said again, louder.

He tried to sit up, but again his body failed to honour his wishes.

"Bronson Timber," she addressed him firmly and, this time, gritted her teeth. "Get the fuck up; we've got to find Dawn. Your pain can wait; push it down and get the fuck up."

He'd never seen her like this. Where had this strength come from? Even the way she stood in front of him was different… she had a confidence that he could only ever dream of. Without thinking, he found he was pulling himself to his feet. He stumbled slightly, and Kenley held out an arm to help.

"Don't help him," she commanded without taking her eyes off her brothers. Kenley retracted his arm just as quickly, as if he'd just placed it in a fire.

Bronson straightened himself up, wiped away his tears and took a deep breath.

"Now, if you want to be a good brother, let's find Dawn, and let's do it now."

18

The Plan

Fleta had spent so much of her life hiding from what happened to her, filled with shame and anxiety... but her newfound fire was everything she needed to get them all moving again; they had to save Dawn.

She had no idea what had awakened within her. Throwing open the doors on her trauma and letting her brother and Kenley in had meant that she had nothing more to hide, no more hidden secrets; she was laid bare. The moment the reality of what had happened to her left her lips, she had broken down the barriers she'd so carefully erected to protect herself from shame. She still felt the shame, it'd be with her forever, but now she felt like that shame could no longer dictate her actions. She had nothing more to fear.

She'd spent years in abject terror, but now

the avatar of that terror, her uncle, was battered upon the ground in their darkened little terrace. He couldn't hurt her anymore.

Her murder of her uncle was a dark secret that compounded the shame of her abuse. With this weight now lifted, it no longer had a hold on her.

Her entire sense of being was built upon a foundation of anger and resentment, atop which laid the layers of shame and fear. Now that those top layers had dissipated, the anger bubbled to the surface. Shame forced her into hiding, whereas this anger was fuel for action.

The worst things imaginable had already happened to her, and she'd won; she'd defeated her demons. What more could hold her back? She couldn't allow Bronson to become burdened by responsibility in a way that had hamstrung her most of her life, so she pushed him forward. They would save Dawn, together.

The group approached a clearing with a rock at its centre, just like the drawing on the parchment. It was beautiful. The darkening sky was orange above them, and the long grasses within the clearing swayed back and forth with the breeze; it looked almost like one of her imaginary retreats. The central rock was fully enveloped in dark green moss which had sprouted small brightly coloured flowers all across its surface. It had a dreamlike prettiness to it, which was a welcome change from the long shadows and dense foliage of the Wildlands - a diamond in the rough.

"Wait," she said as Kenley and Bronson were following the game trail through to the other side of the clearing. "Let's wait for a second."

"We've got to find her, Flea," Bronson said, not stopping.

"Yes," Fleta said. "I know that. But we need a plan."

Bronson paused and turned to face her; his eyes were still red and puffy.

"We're walking into a trap, aren't we? Why would they leave us a detailed map?"

"They want us to follow," Kenley said, "they're going to be expecting us."

"We can't make a plan until we get there," Bronson argued. "We're blind right now; we don't know what to expect."

"I agree," Fleta said running her fingertips over the flowers adorning the boulder. "We need to communicate, Bron. Talk to Kenley... y'know, in your mind."

Bronson frowned.

"You know what I mean, Bron, as you did earlier... You said you needed to understand if it allowed you to talk only to me or everyone. When you talked to Kenley by the river, you could see him. You said it yourself, you don't know if that's why he could hear you."

"So you want to test it out?" Bronson said, raising an eyebrow.

"I'll go over there," Kenley pointed, just beyond the treeline at the opposite end of the clearing. "That way we won't get any false positives by me hearing you talk so close to me."

Bronson sighed. He still felt uneasy about this ability, she could see it written on his face. Eventually, her brother nodded and turned away, making his way onto the opposite side of the clearing from Kenley. Fleta followed her brother.

When Bronson stepped into the thicket, he turned away from the boulder. Fleta walked around and held his arm to soothe him. Bronson frowned and then strained as he appeared to be forcing out his mind-words.

"Hey," Kenley shouted, "that wasn't nice!"

Bronson smirked, then couldn't stop himself from laughing out loud, "I said 'you couldn't hunt a rabbit in a wooden box'."

Fleta laughed, "he's right, y'know, that wasn't nice."

"I wonder if I can hear him talk back to me; hold on." Bronson closed his eyes again.

Within moments his eyes widened, and then he laughed once more.

Fleta raised an eyebrow, "what happened?"

"He's a cheeky little fucker, I'll tell you that much," Bronson laughed. "I spoke to him, and he spoke back."

Kenley approached with a big grin on his face. She'd not seen him smile properly since before Bronson had absconded the camp that morning, and so much had happened since that she'd forgotten what it looked like. Kenley had the type of smile that could pull you out of despair; it was contagious. Pearly white teeth surrounded by soft brown lips with dimples on either side, his dark hair perfectly framed his unblemished, light brown complexion, with eyes so blue that they invited you in. She smiled back at him without even realising she was doing it.

"So what's this plan, Flea?" Kenley asked.

"Don't call her that," Bronson said, "that name's only for me."

Kenley held his hands up, palms facing towards Bronson. "Sorry, I heard you say it, so I thought it was okay."

"Shut up, Bron," she said sternly, "don't make trouble for no reason."

She looked to Kenley. The familiarity her pet name engendered between them felt warm and safe. Her twin was the only person that had called her by this name, and despite it being something that felt powerful and important between them, she had to admit that it was nice to hear other people say it. Especially other people she cared for. The three of them were now enjoined by knowledge of her childhood; so it felt only fitting that they could work within the bounds of this familiarity with one another.

"I go by Flea now," she declared, adjusting her shoulders and lifting her chin to give her a greater stature. "I can do this, Bron, because it's my name, and I get to choose."

Her brother raised his eyebrows, rubbed his forehead with his thumb and forefinger, and then crossed his arms over his chest.

"Does that mean I can call you 'Bron'?" Kenley asked her brother with a knowing mischievousness.

"Don't push it, hunter boy," Bronson retorted.

Kenley gave a faux sigh before laughing heartily. There was little resistance from the others as they all became swept up in the gaiety.

There was a natural rivalry between the hunters and the lumberers of Penny Grove; hunters believe that their best and most essential resources come from the forest habitats as meat and hide, and even medicine from the plants and fungus. In contrast, the lumberers want to cut it all down, believing that we can get all we need in trade with increased economic gains. Neither party were right, of course, and besides, the hunters were fighting a losing battle; Penny Grove was built on the gains from the lumber trade. In truth, Kenley wasn't a hunter, and Bronson wasn't a lumberer - those were the trades of their families, the same families that had so callously discarded them the moment the fire in the Sanctuary was extinguished. That wouldn't stop any mocking though; so deeply ingrained was this culture within the town that even those peripherally involved chose a 'side' either to espouse the benefits or to antagonise the opposition. Between this group this age-old rivalry was little more than banterous, but elsewhere in the town, this rivalry caused some complex social problems.

As the laughing between them died down, Flea set her mind to telling them the plan.

"Look, there's a lot we don't know yet since we haven't seen the camp, but what we *do* know is they know we're coming," as she spoke, she noticed her two companions were fully engaged; there was not a single doubt in their minds that she was to be listened to. When she realised this, she had to fight a tremor in her voice to continue. "If they know we're coming, then we need to approach quietly, they already have the advantage, and we don't know how big this camp is or how many of them there are. We need to scout and sneak until we can learn more."

"I can move silently through the forest,"

Kenley said. "At least, I think I can; I know how."

"That's better than either of us," Bronson said.

"But Bron, you can talk to us," Flea interjected, "which means you can describe what you see and we can plan from a safe distance."

Kenley jumped in, "when we pass the final landmark on the map, this large knobbly tree-thing, I'll go ahead, and you two wait. I can then learn how far away the camp is and give us the initial layout. Then I'll come back, and then Bronson can go ahead and start scouting and telling us what he sees. I don't want us to accidentally crest a hill and be in the middle of their camp without realising."

"Good idea," Flea said as Bronson nodded along in agreement. "Let's find this tree."

In earnest, the three began following the game trail, weaving through trees, ducking under overgrown thickets, and tiptoeing around mossy rocks.

She was nervous. In the back of her mind, she doubted her newfound confidence. What if she was wrong? What if she was leading them into a trap? She had no real experience in what they were doing; what was she thinking, taking charge? The forest's silence brought her back to her old, meek self; it left too much space for rumination. The warm flushes she experienced while discussing the plan gave way to a cold numbness and caused her extremities to tremble. Her panic rose, and her breathing became erratic, but she still did everything she could to keep the volume low enough not to alert the others to her distress.

"You know, this might be the wrong time to tell you this, but my father never taught me to hunt," Kenley said.

His words startled her out of her panic, and as she noticed his presence alongside her, her breathing steadied. As she processed what he was saying, she could not hide the confusion on her face.

"I mean, I know how to hunt because my dad wrote journals and took notes which I read extensively from cover to cover multiple times. He never taught me because he couldn't stand to be around me." Kenley said. "I'm telling you this because you shared something about your life that you found difficult to talk about, and I'm just doing the same."

She lowered her eyes to the ground. Her panic had subsided; his distraction had worked.

"My father found my mother dead, with me in her arms as a baby, and according to what I learned from Addison and his family, it... broke him. He loved my mother so much that seeing her dead changed him entirely."

"Oh Kenley, I'm sorry to hear about that," Flea said.

"Thing is, it's all I've ever known, and I was so obsessed with hunting and learning everything I could about it because I thought that if I did, he'd finally start treating me like a son instead of what is essentially a pet - I was clothed, well fed, but that was it - I was an obligation to him only. Addison's father probably did more of the 'raising' than my father did; he spent much time on long hunts."

"Amazingly, you've learned all this hunting and tracking stuff by yourself," she said, "I would never have known."

"I wanted you to know this about me because sharing what happened between you and your uncle was the bravest thing I've ever seen, and I wanted to give something of my own, in turn. If everyone shared what they were going through, then the worst things that happened to us probably wouldn't have happened at all."

It *was* brave. She hadn't considered that sharing the worst parts of her childhood would be seen by others as brave. Her propensity to think the worst in every situation trained her to think of her sharing as weak or shameful.

She liked the sound of *brave*.

"I doubted you when I had my vision," he continued. "I didn't understand what I was seeing, or appreciate the context. I'm sorry."

"You don't have to apologise," Flea said, "I know how it probably looked."

"Having that doubt has taught me an important lesson about these visions," he said. "I can't always draw conclusions from what I'm seeing. It's tough... really tough... especially when what I'm seeing looks so... complete."

She nodded along with him.

"It means I need to give Dawn the benefit of the doubt based on what I saw of her too," Kenley said. "I don't know what led up to what I saw, I only saw the aftermath."

Flea caught Kenley's eyes, and they smiled softly at each other as they walked.

"My illness over the past day or so was withdrawal from gravel," Bronson said. "My uncle got me addicted to it. I looked up to him, and everyone in the Grove loved him, but behind closed doors, instead of looking after us, he raped my sister and got me, as a child, addicted to drugs."

"Thanks for sharing–" Kenley started, before Bronson cut him off.

"I'm not sharing for us all to pat ourselves on our backs about our traumas; I'm sharing so that you know I'm serious when I tell you I'll do anything to protect my sister; I have to protect her to make up for everything, and I will spend every waking moment doing just that."

Despite being a few steps ahead of her, Flea could tell he was talking through gritted teeth.

He stopped, turned, and levelled a stare directly at Kenley, "and also for you to know it doesn't matter how trustworthy everyone else thinks you are, I won't trust you, and I won't trust anyone else, when it comes to my sister and me."

"What are you saying, Bron?" Flea asked.

"I can see what's happening here between you two," he looked back and forth between Flea and Kenley, with his eyes lowered in suspicion. "I'm just making some things clear. There is nobody in this world that'll get in my way, with protecting my sister. I will not let your friendship alter my plans."

Then he turned and resumed walking, and their silent march towards the gnarled tree from the parchment continued.

Flea shook her head as she considered his comments. Other people have controlled too much of her life, and whilst she loved her brother, she wouldn't trade her uncles control for her brothers. She was the only person who would decide what she wanted in life, not her Uncle, not her parents, and certainly not Bronson. It was her right to decide how to act.

She couldn't put her foot down with Bronson

right now though, she couldn't make her views known. She wouldn't risk conflict, and they couldn't afford to lose trust in one another. If they did, she knew that whatever was to come next, they would need to pay a heavy price.

19

Execution

Dawn was floating on an endless sea of darkness, her entire body ached, and hope was not forthcoming. In her imaginings, it was not Addison that came to her heroic rescue, but Bronson, with a strength that mirrored her own during the fight against the brothers, dashing her poor captors upon the rocks as a furious blackened wave in this deep void of emptiness within her mind.

The icy water brought her out of the darkness as it splashed upon her face. Her eyes crept open letting in blinding rays of orange light.

"Wakey, wakey," a familiar voice said. "It's time to wake up, sweetheart."

This gentleness encouraged her to open her eyes some more and brought into focus the bruised visage of Brother Yuri. The memories of her encounter with Brother Alex and his companions rushed back to her. All she could taste was iron, and a scent of wood burning permeated her senses.

"Wakey, wakey," he said once more.

She shook off the remaining darkness and composed herself.

She was bound tightly.

She struggled, but as she did, she felt pressure at her throat.

"I wouldn't do that if I were you," Brother Yuri said.

"What's happened?" her voice was hoarse and quiet.

"Well, you've *awakened*; that's what's happened."

"Of course, you threw water on me," she quipped through gritted teeth.

"You're awake, sure... but you've become awakened." The words slipped out of him slowly, as if he was asking her to really comprehend their meaning.

"Awakened," she mused, "what do you mean?"

"Come on, dear," he said, as if exhausted by her question. "You're a scholar of the Book, you know what I'm talking about. You're awakened, you're an abomination."

An abomination.

The word drove a spike of coldness right through her chest, and the feeling radiated outwards from her heart, chilling her bones across the breadth of her bound body.

The term 'abomination' was used extensively in the Book of Inauron to classify and admonish those who refused to relinquish their powers, as Inauron once did. But those were just stories, fables to teach morality. The magical powers detailed in the book, as she understood it, were allegories for the powers of greed, political power, false piety and other such sins.

She gulped, widening her eyes, as she struggled against her bindings once more, but Yuri placed a hand upon her shoulder.

"Don't struggle, just be patient, I'll explain it all," Brother Yuri said warmly. Given her situation, she wondered about his tone and why was he being kind to her. Was it in jest? A mockery? "First, let me explain your bindings in case you accidentally kill yourself."

The colour drained from her, and as if sensing her unease, he elaborated.

"Don't worry; these bindings are completely harmless if you follow the rules," he said, smiling warmly. "You've awakened, an abomination, one that can draw upon unnatural strength. These bindings have been designed across centuries, specifically to contain those of your particular affliction. You'll notice your hands are pulled behind your back, and your legs are affixed to the ground. All the bindings are connected; it's a single rope. Pulling at one end tightens the other."

He paused to allow her to comprehend his words.

"One thing I suspect you haven't yet noticed, is the blade pointing upwards tied against your breasts. Tightening your bindings brings the blade to your throat. Continuing to struggle at this point is fatal. The more strength you draw upon to free yourself, the hastier your demise."

Her eyes fell to her chest, but she couldn't tilt her head down far enough to see it; the bindings that held her hands and feet had pulled her posture backwards, so she was almost looking towards the evening sky.

"It is what we must do to contain one of seemingly unlimited strength, we cannot possibly face you, toe to toe, so we must instead use our heads, to ensnare you and trap you in a binding that penalises your use of this strength."

She closed her eyes, fully understanding the peril she was in. If she struggled, the knife would pierce her throat. She thought about pulling the bindings apart quickly, but she worried that would shoot the knife through her at a comparable speed to her use of strength. She was well and truly contained.

"On our journey, you spoke much of your kinship with the Sanctuary and your training to become a devotee; so I assume you're fully aware of what an abomination is and what it represents."

"Someone who refused to give up their power," she answered, "but I don't have power."

"Ah, my four deceased brothers would disagree with that assessment," he interlocked his fingers and dropped his head.

"I saved you from them."

"I thank you for your gesture of goodness, dear Dawn. Alas, it was founded upon a lie; I was not running from them," his head tilted in sympathy, and the gesture angered her; he was taking her for a fool.

"Are you even blind?"

"In a matter of speaking," he said, and she noticed his mouth tilt momentarily into a smirk, before returning to neutrality. "I can see... but differently from you. I see your aura. I see it inflaming as you anger. The clearest thing I see are your powers as you use them, you're bright like the flaming sun, illuminating all around you."

The fires that he spoke of, those burning within her, became hotter, and without thinking, she twisted her arms against the bindings at her wrists. She felt them tightening in response and the blade inched closer. She knew she needed to somehow gain full control of her rising temper before the knife reached her throat. She exhaled loudly in resignation and followed it with calming breaths.

His voice softened once more, as he spoke, "I want you to know that these little lies are necessary, and if you give me a moment to explain, I'll certainly be able to put your mind at ease."

She breathed out, calming herself.

"We are adherents to the law set forth by the Brothers of Inauron. We are separate from the Church of Inauron; we operate independently, and it's our sole charge to keep abominations at bay. We are all here in these forsaken wilds because of you children. We've been given the… admittedly very tough job of attempting to corral you together. Though we didn't expect you'd split up. We had placed our hopes upon a sense of teenage camaraderie, and that you'd all stay together; small-town spirit and all that. This was the reason for my deception, I needed to convince you to join me, and once you'd joined with us, Brother Alex and his team would take over and attempt to lure your companions in."

"Why are you telling me all this?"

"You said you're training to become a

devotee," he said in a way that clearly made more sense to him than it did to Dawn. "We're on the same side. Our interests are with the sanctity of the Church, which I'm certain you agree is the law absolute."

"How can I be an abomination?" she could not stop her bottom lip from trembling. He was implying that she was the very thing she'd been taught to avoid; prideful politicians, ego-driven members of the constabulary who give no inch to their authority, criminals with an empire they refuse to relinquish, and any others who refused to acquiesce during the revolutions eight hundred years ago. "I hold no power, I'm nothing like those in the stories; I'm just a girl from a town in the middle of nowhere with nothing to my name but what my family allows me."

He chuckled, and she frowned.

"Modern interpretations of the Book of Inauron are certainly lacking the flavour of the original..." his warm smile was disarming, but she needed to keep her mind on understanding what was happening to her. "You are taught that the power that makes an abomination is authority and control, and it's interpreted that way since we Brothers do such good work keeping you away from the true understanding and the definition of power as it was originally written. This was, of course, a necessary change in interpretation. We work so hard to keep knowledge of the real abominations away from the public, by suppressing and eliminating them as they appear... so it left the fear associated by encountering one - such as yourself - lacking in its ability to drive positive behaviour change."

"Let me ask you this," he continued, "in what world can a petite, pretty little thing like you, utterly destroy four adult men, one of which was as large as a mountain?"

He raised his eyebrow while waiting for a response, but she had none. Her recollection of what had occurred with Brother Alex was hazy, and what she *did* remember was traumatic. She can still smell their blood, see flashes of torn flesh, and feel the slick warmth of their blood between her fingertips.

"I watched it," he continued, placing a finger upon his lips as he considered his words carefully. "You were like a whirlwind of death, bouncing from victim to victim, leaving destruction in your wake."

"This is power," he said. "This was the original definition of an abomination. You exhibited a power we've not seen for many, many years, but thankfully for us all, it's a power that we Brothers are trained to manage."

"I don't want this power; take it from me," she said, tears welling up.

"Would that I could, little lamb."

"Inauron gave up his power and used the rest of his life helping others; give me that opportunity," she cried.

He smiled sympathetically.

"Unfortunately, this is another divergence between the original Book and the modern version. The Inauron sacrificed himself publically, and in doing so, he galvanised the revolution. He didn't just hand over his power like a market transaction."

Sacrificed himself?

"No, you're wrong," she cried, "why would the stories get this wrong? It's the main crux of the faith."

"The Church does what it needs to in its interpretations of the Book of Inauron, but each divergence from the original makes our job a little more difficult. Hundreds of years ago, communities would oust abominations from their midst themselves; now it's down to us to do that difficult job."

"How did I get this power? What happened to me?" Tears were now flowing freely down her cheeks. "What are you going to do to me?"

"Calm yourself, Dawn, your upset causes you to forget the bindings. We need you alive."

There was no stopping her pain; Brother Yuri had just told her she was the antithesis of all she'd been taught and that there was no way to reverse it.

"What do you do with abominations?" she cried out.

"I don't want to lie to you even more than necessary, Dawn, but I'll tell you this, as far as the Church is concerned, there were ten children trapped inside the Sanctuary and none made it out alive. It's our job to make reality fit the story."

So they would all be killed.

Executed.

"You said you needed me alive!" she bellowed between sobs.

"Yes," he said softly. "You're our bait for the others."

He stood and walked away, handing the guard duty to one of the other Brothers.

He turned, looking back at her bound form, "Brother Sloane will look after you whilst we wait for your friends."

The hulking, robed figure walked over to her, crouched down, leaned close to her ear and said gruffly, "you killed my brother, let's see if we can do something about that..."

20

The Camp Site

Kenley pushed through the undergrowth slowly, returning to the gnarled tree just off the game trail. There he saw Flea and Bronson, stood in a familial embrace.

"The campsite is about a four or five minutes walk that way," he said.

They turned to face him.

Flea wiped at her eyes and stood confidently.

"Bron, over to you," she instructed.

Her brother nodded and approached Kenley.

"What can I expect?"

"It's a small camp; I didn't see Dawn, but there were two canvas tents and a small fire; she may have been inside one of the tents."

"How many people are there?"

"I saw just one from where I was, tending the fire, but I had an obscured view; it'd be better if you scout about and see if you can see anything else."

Bronson nodded again and approached the thicket Kenley had just emerged from. He was nervous about this; he had his reservations. Kenley was far more adept at sneaking, but he had to admit his ability to describe what he sees puts him at an advantage. He knew that Fleta and Kenley could put together a plan of action, whilst he was overseeing the camp, as he communicated back and forth with the detail of what he was seeing. It wasn't the best plan, but he could at least see the logic. Still, he wasn't the lithest of movers; even without the occasional tremor of withdrawal he still felt every few minutes.

Before he lost sight of the tree, Flea called out to him.

"Tell us everything you see; if something goes wrong, we'll come running." He kept his eyes upon hers as she spoke, "be safe, please."

He ducked beneath a low branch and made his way along Kenley's path.

He walked along the side of a steep banking; trees jutted out of the slope at odd angles, at no less density than on the flatter ground. He had to watch his step. He surmised that based on this path, he'd be high enough to look down upon this small camp when he eventually reached it.

The darkness within the brush was palpable; even without the dimness of the evening sky, the density of the foliage meant that he could barely see more than maybe two or three trees deep from where he stood. It was isolating. He looked back and could no longer see the gnarled landmark tree where his sister waited, and he couldn't yet see the campsite ahead. Nothing told him he was on the right path; he had to trust his steps, and Kenley's directions.

As he trudged across the slope, stepping over horizontal tree trunks and rocks, he thought about the last few days.

Everyone around him had changed irreparably. Addison who doted on Dawn had inexplicably left her alone, Kenley who spent all his time shying away in Addison's shadow had developed the uncanny ability to track people and somehow see the future; he himself had found the ability to talk across impossible distances, Dawn could kill and mutilate four adult men single-handedly, and Fleta his meek, quiet sister had become strong, confident... and a killer to-boot. Everything he knew about these people, even those closest to him had changed. He considered whether the personalities he saw today were their 'real' personalities that he'd been too high on gravel to see before now, or if perhaps everyone was different since the night of the fire.

He ducked under a protruding branch, walked beneath the torn roots of a tree that had fallen against the slope, and crept across the surface of a mossy rock. The air had a distinct chill, and he waited in the coolness to see if he could sense any movement or light from this supposed camp ahead.

Something flickered on the forest floor some metres below him, and he craned his neck to get a better look. It was a small fire that cast enough light in the darkened woods to see, despite its distance.

He slowly descended the slope closer to the light, vying to see more.

"I see the fire," he said through his mind to his sister.

"Slowly now," she reminded him, "don't get seen."

From where he crouched on the slope, he looked down upon a camp with two canvas tents, a fire, and a single man stoking the flames with a stick. It was exactly as Kenley described, but he still couldn't see Dawn. She must be inside one of the tents; there was nowhere else for her to be. The man stoking the fire was elderly, with wrinkles across his leathern face and a large bruise that occupied much of his visage... he wore the same clothing as those four bodies.

"I see one man," he said to his sister across the void.

"There has to be more somewhere," she said, "maybe they're gathering firewood or something; keep your wits about you."

He crept about the slope, encircling the camp below until he was near its rear. He still could not see anyone except the elderly man near the fire. That man appeared to pose no threat to him. Bronson knew he wasn't the strongest of people, more tall and lean than muscular, but this ancient man looked like he would snap at a wrong look. He was certain if he took the man by surprise, he could get him to free Dawn.

"I'm going in," he said to his sister.

"Bronson don't do anything stupid; we're here to plan, not act."

"It's one guy; I can take him. If Dawn's not there, we can do a prisoner swap."

"I don't think this is a good idea; please come back."

"I'll go quiet for a bit, and once I've subdued him, I'll report back."

He closed his mind off to her protestations as he crept towards the base of the slope. He was determined to be the one that saved Dawn. He needed a win, he needed something to prove that he could be the protector he should have been with his sister all along. This is the thought that he kept in mind as he approached the camp's rear, behind the two canvas tents. He was crouched, trying to keep as low a profile as possible, creeping between the tents, nearing the elderly man's back.

"Ah, Bronson, I presume," the voice flooded his mind.

He froze.

"Please, sit at the fire with me," the voice commanded. "I've been waiting on your arrival."

He didn't know what to do; he hadn't thought this possible. Somehow this man was talking to him like he talked to Fleta - directly into his mind. He felt the chill from the air ever more keenly, as his face flushed.

"I have meat," the man said aloud as he turned, showing the skinned rabbit he had roasting over the flames. "Please sit; I'm of no threat to you... but you already know that, don't you."

He hesitated, then slowly made his way to the fire and sat. He brought his knees up to his face, hiding his embarrassment.

"She's not here by the way," the man said aloud but calmly. "The 'real' camp is a little further back that way."

He pointed behind the tents, "this was just a decoy... for you."

Bronson tensed up, and the elderly man,

sensing this, spoke with a smile designed to ease his nerves, "don't worry, this isn't an ambush; nobody is waiting in the wings to jump out and take you captive."

"Where's Dawn?"

"She's safe, relatively unharmed, though that's more than I can say for four of my Brothers."

Bronson's eyes dropped to the ground; he'd seen those Brothers, those mutilated forms spread across the forest floor, he could still smell the dankness of the torn flesh and blood.

"She's no longer the Dawn you know," he continued.

"What do you mean?"

He pushed his fingers into the rabbit's meat, and pulled a piece free, handing it to Bronson, then took some himself.

"Think about it. Since you've been out here, has anything remained the same? Are you the same? Your sister? Kenley?"

As if the man had mined Bronson's apprehensions, he faced down the very idea he'd ruminated over only moments ago. The rabbit was mouthwatering; he'd not eaten in far too long. The elderly man passed him some more meat torn from the freshly cooked carcass which he took with an eagerness that betrayed his reservations about the man.

"Twas the fire in the Sanctuary," he said. "It changed everyone."

Bronson frowned; this man knew too much, and he didn't know what his game was. He wished he had the wit to contend with him, but he listened instead and took in what he was being told.

"I'm Brother Yuri," he said. "Apologies for not introducing myself sooner, I forget myself."

Before Bronson could reply, the man continued, "when Sanctuary trees become damaged, it's our job to clean up the fallout. The tree is important, you see. It's a ward, a protection against an affliction."

"Affliction?" Bronson gulped, hanging on the man's every word.

"Unfortunately yes, a disease that rots the mind and body... you have it, your sister has it, and I'm sorry to tell you that everyone in Penny Grove has it too. If they're not dead already, they will be, shortly."

He trembled.

"The moment this disease begins to take hold, people tend to do things so vastly out of character that it becomes abundantly clear there's no hope."

"What do you mean?"

"I urge you to recall a time when your sister would have the strength of will to murder your uncle. I would suggest that this event in itself is out of character, wouldn't you?"

"He abused her for years," he spat, not wanting to believe it.

"Did he? Or is that just what she told you?"

He felt anger burning in his chest; he gritted his teeth and clenched his fist.

"I see you don't like what I'm saying, but consider for a moment that I may be right," the man held his arms open in a welcoming gesture, "wouldn't you want to know if you were being led down the wrong path? Manipulated?"

He wouldn't entertain the idea that his sister had lied, he couldn't do that to himself, and he couldn't do it to her. This man was a snake, a viper, here to poison his thoughts and turn them against each other.

"I believe her every word," he retorted.

"And so you should, as a loving brother," the man quipped. "Perhaps it's worth considering then, how your childhood crush could overpower four of my Brothers. I assume you've seen the bodies; else, how would you have found your way to my camp?"

Bronson nodded.

"Is that the Dawn you know? The cold-blooded killer?"

His eyes pointed to the ground again, the

man's words were making sense, and he hated it. Dawn was different, Fleta was different, but that didn't mean they were afflicted, or dying, or whatever else Brother Yuri was implying.

"In truth, and I appreciate this is likely exceptionally hard to hear," he raised his eyebrows sympathetically. "All ten of you perished in spirit during the fire. What's left now, are these dangerous husks that must be captured. I'm not evil; I'm not out here hunting children like some callous villain... I'm trying to prevent the spread of a disease that could corrupt the entire world."

"What do you mean perished in spirit? My sister is no longer herself?"

"Has she changed? Does she have the same mannerisms and personality traits that she had before the fire? Is she stronger mentally? Physically?"

Bronson closed his eyes for a moment.

Brother Yuri continued, "I represent an order called the Brothers of Inauron, and it's our job to fix all the problems associated with the failure of Sanctuary wards. Unfortunately, there's no known cure for the affliction, so we're dispatched to ensure the disease doesn't spread."

"How come you're not afflicted?"

"I am... as are you," he replied quickly. "The disease manifests in many forms, the mildest of which is called Cogitauron. This type cannot spread, provided those afflicted are correctly managed. This is what I have, and you do too."

"How do you know this?"

"Because we can do this," he said directly into Bronson's mind. "I know you can too; I've been listening."

His blood ran cold. He could hear Bronson the whole time; he knew of the plan to sneak up on him; he knew everything...

"How do you know all this? About me, about Fleta and Uncle Javi? Where are you getting your information?"

"This power we share gives us certain advantages," he said. "We arrived in Penny Grove forty strong. Only ten of us were dispatched to the Wildlands to capture you children. The others are interrogating your parents, your peers, your rivals... and that information is simply communicated directly to us as we need it."

Ten in the Wildlands... that meant that besides Brother Yuri and the four deceased Brothers, that there were another five. He needed to tell Fleta, but Brother Yuri was listening. He was suddenly exposed and could do nothing to ease his mind.

"What now?"

Brother Yuri pressed his lips together in a

sympathetic gesture.

"You'll be given a choice, of course. It was the choice all of my brothers had been given. We're all similarly afflicted, Cogitaurons, the lot of us. You can join the Brothers of Inauron, be welcomed into the fold as Brother..."

"And the other option?"

"You'll be executed when the time is right, along with your peers," Brother Yuri said softly, in a way that felt painfully at odds with the words he spoke.

"So everyone's going to die?"

He'd lost energy to contend with this man; the information he was given was too heavy, too life-changing. He couldn't deny the truth in what this man was saying, but he didn't want to give up on his sister; he couldn't.

"The moment the fire broke out, your sister died, as did Dawn, as did everyone else," he said. "Who they are now is of no consequence. Your sister, the child you loved, is already dead; you, Bronson, are already dead. But this opportunity, this choice, will allow you to live in the grace of the Church with a singularly important mission."

He felt nausea building, and a chill upon his extremities.

"Will you join us, Bronson? Will you help us save the world?"

21

An Uncomfortable Sight

Flea rushed through the brush, cutting herself on the thickets and leaping over fallen trees. Her stupid brother had ruined their plans, and now she had no idea where he was. Kenley followed closely, trying in vain to get her to slow down.

"We're getting close; hold up," he called after her, hoping the density of the woods would dampen his voice. "We don't want to give away our position."

She didn't slow down; she kept pushing forward, desperate to fix her brother's mess. His silence scared her; why wouldn't he talk to her?

"There," she said, pointing down the steep slope towards the campsite. She didn't see anyone there but didn't wait to assess the scene before hurtling toward the smouldering fire.

Kenley slid down the hill on his rear, utilising the detritus to smooth his path as he raced to catch up with a frenzied Flea.

She reached the camp and looked around, seeing nobody. Then she turned and whipped open the canvas flaps of the two tents, revealing their emptiness. The fire was still hot but was no longer burning; she kicked at the coals in frustration, sending hot embers flying around in a wide arc in front of her.

"He's done something stupid, I'm sure of it," she said, panting.

Kenley placed a comforting hand on her upper back, but she shrugged it off before staring at him, brow furrowed.

"Sorry, I was just trying to..."

"Just... don't," she dismissed his apology before he could finish it. She was in no mood for niceties; her brother and his sheer idiocy consumed her thoughts.

"I can't believe he'd try something without letting us know," she threw her arms in the air. "We had a plan - sure it wasn't the best plan in the world, but the least he could do was stick to it."

Kenley didn't know what to say; he just tried to make himself look busy by checking the tents once more and then wandering the perimeter to find out where Bronson went.

"There are footsteps in the mud here, leading

that way," he pointed north.

"Then, let's go," Flea started.

"Wait," he said firmly, halting her advance.

She crossed her arms and turned slowly to face him.

"Let's take a breath. We have no idea what we're about to run into, and if you sprint ahead, you might find yourself in more trouble than we can handle."

She knew he was right, but that didn't stop the impulse to jump fully into her fate to find her brother. Her heart beat within her chest and the rising desperation was a difficult beast to tame.

"It was your caution that made us late to find him in the first place," she said. "When Bron told us what he was doing, you said to wait, be patient, and now look what's happened."

He rubbed at his temple and winced, "What if Bronson was following the plan, as we agreed, and you rushed in prematurely, putting him in danger?"

She rolled her eyes, knowing he was right, but she had far too much energy burning within her breast just to let things lie and accept Bronson's fate.

"How was I supposed to know Bronson had gone off the script?"

Kenley closed his eyes and pointed his

eyebrows at the centre as if he was willing away some sensation Flea could not place. His breathing became sporadic.

Her demeanour softened, "are you okay?"

"I'm..."

"Is it happening again? The visions, I mean?"

He nodded, then fell to a knee.

She rushed to him, not knowing how to support him, but she did her best to keep him upright as he lost his balance.

"Ken, talk to me; what's happening," she gasped, panicking.

"My head," he breathed.

As he turned his head to meet her gaze, she saw blood beginning to pool at the corners of his eyes.

"Try... ummm...," she lost her words as she tried desperately to find something to help. She thought back to all the worst moments in her life and how despite the injustice of what was happening to her, it was safer at the moment just to let it happen, to loosen the reins of control, to find a way herself in a position where she could drift off to one of her beautiful little imaginary retreats; the fields of swaying grass and serene clifftop views bathed in sunlight. "Try to let it take over, don't fight it."

She wasn't sure he could hear her; sweat was

glistening upon his unblemished tan forehead.

"Let it take you over, Ken," she said, louder this time. She pushed him backwards gently, setting him upon the ground, then lay him back upon the soft bedding of the forest floor. "Let it happen, don't fight."

She could see as his breathing became more regular and his eyelids slowly lowered into slumber. It was working; it was helping. His breathing slowed once more and his eyes shot open, revealing eyeballs entirely coloured the same milky white she saw during his last vision. However, this time, he was not strained; he looked relaxed and comfortable, as if allowing the vision to guide him, like driftwood upon a choppy sea.

All she could do now was wait.

She held his hand and momentarily placed her other upon his chest, feeling his heart beat slowly. Her pale thumb smoothed the caramel skin of his hand as she held it softly.

She gulped in anticipation of his waking - what would he see this time?

The silence in the forest seemed overwhelmingly loud, and as her anxiety grew, she rubbed her thumb against his hand with less comforting movements. His steady breathing had taken on a raspy texture as if he needed to clear his throat; she rubbed his hand with her thumb more recklessly.

Her mind wandered in the silence. It was what she was most afraid of; being left alone with her thoughts. As if she'd taken on Kenley's own panic, allowing him to settle but unwittingly burdening her with more frayed and tangled nerves than her mind could handle. She felt as if she were drowning. She directed her energy at Kenley's sleeping form, willing him to wake up with stares, but he stayed still. She tried to remember the last time it happened and wondered how long it had been, but in her panic, she had no idea how much time had already passed. Had it been seconds or minutes?

Flea exhaled and found scant comfort in the sound of her breath, breaking through the silence that plagued her. She tried to breathe louder, hoping the sound would distract her from the maelstrom of thoughts overpowering her consciousness. Eventually, however, she spoke aloud, telling the spirits of nature all of her ills.

"Every time I think I'm safe, I'm reminded how I'm not in the most upsetting ways," she started, speaking between erratic breaths in an uncontrolled manner. "A childhood of trauma finally resolved by killing my abuser, but we're banished before I can rest. Separating from a life I hated, I was optimistic about what came next, and my brother immediately fell ill and disappeared. Finding my brother and losing Dawn; getting close to Kenley but pushing him away; making a solid plan to rescue Dawn, but Bronson breaks it to go off on his own."

She held a hand across her stomach as she felt sickened by everything that had happened, "one step forward, one step back. I'm destined to be chasing my tail. I just want happiness..."

Tears trickled down from her deep blue eyes, "I thought becoming Flea would fix everything... I wanted desperately to be the person I always should have been if it wasn't for Javi. Flea is strength, confidence, and aggression, but Fleta is a nervous wreck, incapable of happiness. I so desperately wanted to be Flea, who had taken her future into her own hands, to embody the strength that allowed me to fix my problems..."

She looked around theatrically, "but I must admit that the only person here is Fleta; the broken one. What am I even doing here? What can I possibly hope to achieve? I can't save Dawn and now Bronson. I'm a nobody. I can't fix any of my problems."

Tears had left rivulets in the dirt that had stained her cheeks throughout the last few days as she wept loudly. She'd spent so much energy trying to suppress her emotions and control her surroundings; now that the gates had been opened, the floods were forthcoming.

She felt Kenley's grip on her hand tighten

briefly before he sat up and put his arms around her; the jolt of shock warmed her body. She shook beneath his embrace, partly because of her outpouring of emotion and partly because of her resistance to being held. Still, as he held her, the urge to sink her weeping eyes into his comforting shoulder overcame her. He had heard too much; the worry of him seeing the 'real' Fleta sickened her, and she reddened. Letting him see her in this state was a far bigger ill than her usually uncompromising aversion to touch was within her, and so she held him tightly.

She regained control of her breathing and her tears. She attempted to rebuild the surrounding walls that had kept her safe all these years, but he spoke, ruining all her progress.

"I heard enough to feel some of your heartache," he started softly, warmly, "you're not two people. Flea is Fleta, and Fleta is Flea."

His voice was barely more than a whisper, but it felt as though he spoke directly into her soul.

"You are the one that killed your sick abuser; you had no qualms about charging into the forest to find your brother this morning; you are the one that put together the plan to rescue Dawn. You are the one that found the strength to share with me and your brother the most horrific story of your childhood," he paused, "and you are the one who had the power to endure all that pain to protect your family."

"You are not weak. You can't hide behind another name, hoping to give it a new personality - every trait you see in Flea exists within Fleta right now, and every trait you see in Fleta exists within Flea too, you are one and the same. This is why you're special. You can endure so much and still come out the other side caring for others more than yourself. You always put others first."

She no longer had the power to put her guard up to protect herself. He was striking a chord with her in a way nobody had before.

"You've not eaten or drunk anything all day because you've always had people to save and battles to fight. Worthy battles, I might add. Your own needs always come after others."

He pulled back, placing a hand on each of her shoulders to look into her eyes, but she lowered her head, hiding as well as she could. He didn't stop speaking; his words were a dagger straight into her defences. His voice became less pointed but more comforting and familiar.

"Before we were exiled, I didn't know you; I'd only admired you from afar. Hearing how you characterised yourself just now differs completely from the Fleta I see. You called yourself incapable of happiness, broken, and a nervous wreck, but that's not what I see. I see someone who would stop at nothing to save everyone around them; a champion, a hero. Granted, a hero that's been through a very difficult upbringing, but a hero nonetheless."

"Heroes are like clay," he continued, "you can form them however you need to, but until they've been fired, they can deform and collapse at any moment. You've been through that fire and endured that pain, so you're already the complete hero... and I'll always be here supporting you."

He pulled her close once more and held her. The comfort it gave her couldn't quell her deep unconscious aversion to being touched, and as that aversion reached a fever pitch, she could do nothing to stop herself from pushing him away. He didn't fight it, as if he knew it was coming. The guilt washed over her the moment they parted; he was trying his hardest to help her, but she just couldn't let him in.

"I'm here whenever you want me to be. I'm going to be your supporter from now right until the point you tell me to stop." He smiled as she locked eyes with him, "If you want to spend that time hugging or pushing me away, that's fine by me. I'm here for you."

She took a deep breath inward and wiped the tears that had run wild across her face, regaining her composure. She hadn't stopped the shakes, like an internal vibration she couldn't prevent, but as she exhaled, she felt the warmth returning to her fingers. Fleta looked to the sky as she breathed a few times slowly, and carefully.

The silence in the air no longer pained her.

She levelled a stare right at Kenley.

"Thank you."

Just as she rose from the dirt, she remembered why they were on the ground; her heart fluttered, and her stomach sank.

His vision.

"What did you see?"

His eyes flicked towards the ground.

"We need to talk about your brother."

22

Bound

Brother Sloane bent to lift a mossy log that lay near the canvas tent they'd erected for Dawn. One end of it was stuck in the dirt and left a small trench along the soft ground as the hulking figure pulled it over to her. A deep, earthy thud rang out as the log crashed to the ground. The oversized Brother stepped over and then dropped their body onto it to sit before her.

Brother Sloane slowly reached up and pulled back the hooded robe exposing their face. *Her* face. Dawn's eyes widened; given her size and gruff voice, she'd fully accepted this figure before her was male.

"Let's have a little chat," Sloane said. Dawn remembered seeing Brother Cillian's cold stare from across the river, and could see the familial resemblance in the stare levelled at her from Sloane. Whilst her brow was softer, her stare was no less intense. Cillian's stare was authoritative, whereas Sloane's gave her an air of unpredictability that scared Dawn to the core.

"Are you going to hurt me?"

"Y'know, of the pair of us, Cillian was the fighter. I'm more of a talker." She took a long breath and Dawn could see her pained expression as she mentioned her brother. "I used to get us in trouble with my mouth, and he used to get us out of it with his fists. We had a good dynamic."

"I'm sorry about your brother," Dawn said quietly.

"It doesn't matter, it's done," she sighed. "Now if it were me you killed, then I'm certain Cillian would take great pleasure in causing you pain as revenge. I'm different though, I won't be hurting ya."

Dawn breathed a sigh of relief, the pain she was already feeling in her extremities from the ropes was more than enough for her to take already.

As if detecting her relief, Sloane continued, "don't misunderstand me, girl. You'll be hurt, it just won't be me that's doing it."

Dawn shivered as the cold bit at her extremities, "what do you mean?"

"See, the thing about your unique set of

restraints is that all I need to do is find the right combination of words to get you to struggle, and that knife will make it's way to your throat," she paused, "and I'm confident you'll react."

She steeled herself for the inevitable onslaught that Brother Sloane was certain to orchestrate, carefully tightening her fists without straining against the tension of the ropes.

"I'm confident in your death, because in all my years of doing this, I've never met a Furauron without an anger problem," she showed her teeth as she coldly smirked.

"What did you call me?" Dawn asked, partly because the word Brother Sloane used confused her, and partly because she knew she must take whatever opportunity she had to deflect and misdirect. She couldn't let Sloane get her claws into her.

"A Furauron; it's the word for Aurons with your... particular affliction. An Auron of Fury. There's something to be said about that," she mused, whilst adjusting her stocky frame upon the log, "is it a predisposition for anger that causes this fury disease to take, or is it the other way 'round? We'll never know for certain because of the inherent risk of keeping Furaurons alive. I guess I'll see if I can learn what I can whilst I'm here."

The words were alien to Dawn but she

recognised that Brother Sloane must be a scholar of some kind. Brother Yuri had kept it simple, but the musings and expressions Sloane used gave Dawn the impression that she was academic - she reminded Dawn of some of the devotees in Penny Grove's Sanctuary.

"I guess we'll find out if we can trigger this sense of anger y'have swirling around inside you," she eased herself into a more comfortable seating position upon the mossy log.

Dawn stayed silent as she became overwhelmed by the whole situation.

"Let's start with your family…"

Dawn's eyebrow raised.

"Did your father beat you as a child?"

"No." Her response was immediate, but a lie. Her father wasn't cruel, but he was strict. An authoritarian who commanded respect in their family. He'd had big plans for Dawn's life, whether Dawn wanted them, or not.

Sloane smiled. "How often did he beat you?"

"I said he didn't."

"Your mouth did, but your body did not."

She clenched her teeth and tightened her fists. She would talk through her anger, it was the only way she knew to process it.

"Why do they call you Brother, when you're female like me?"

"Am I?" Sloane cocked her head back and laughed. "You are correct. 'Brother' is a title. Our organisation was started around five hundred years ago by three actual familial brothers and one friend. They learned early on that the friend was often excluded from discussions or decisions, just by virtue of the fact that they didn't all share the same bond. Recognising this early, they formally inducted themselves into a new family, one without blood bonds. 'Brother' was the title they used when they all welcomed each other into this new family. This became tradition. Blood bonds none of us; except of course for Cillian and myself, we joined together. You ended that, of course…. Now, how often did your father beat you?"

Dawn had hoped that engaging Sloane would divert her attention from the questioning, but she now feared that she was unnecessarily prolonging the inquisition.

"Only when I needed it."

"Interesting." She placed a hand on her chin, "did you need it often?"

"What does 'often' mean?"

"Daily?"

"No."

"Weekly?"

"Perhaps."

"Is he quick to anger, your father?"

"He can be."

"So you have an anger problem, and your father has an anger problem. Perhaps you are predisposed to becoming a Furauron. Your fate appears set in stone, dear Dawn."

She knew that if she was going to come out of this alive; she needed to continue the back-and-forth; she needed to bat questions back at Sloane so that the silence between them gave her the opportunity to calm her rising temper - she needed time and space to calm herself, and if Sloane's volleys were rapid, Dawn wouldn't be afforded that time.

"What's an Auron?" she asked.

Sloane smiled, perhaps recognising Dawn's intention, or perhaps relishing the opportunity to talk about her interests. "Abomination we call them, as per the Book. Though in truth you are an Auron; a member of the people who came before the Church. The Inauron himself was an Auron - the clue is in the name."

"Why do you call him 'the' Inauron, and not just Inauron, like we do?"

"Because we know the truth; that 'Inauron' as a word, meant someone who sacrifices their Aura, and the story of the Book of Inauron was centred around the first, but not the only Inauron." She paused, and as the quiet settled around them, she leaned forward and spoke with a directness she'd not yet exhibited. "You will become an Inauron once we gather your friends."

"A sacrifice?"

Sloane nodded.

"I learned so much about the Church, and it was all based on the Book of Inauron, which you're telling me is now inaccurate? Or is it just plain wrong?"

Her interrogator shrugged, "not wrong. Reinterpreted."

She clarified, "over generations, the likelihood of an Auron appearing dipped to such a level that the word itself became obsolete, except for those of us who like to research the millennia-old tomes of the previous age. So 'Inauron' lost its connection to the word 'Auron' and then, 'Inauron' was adjusted to become a name and not a descriptor. The story evolved as the world changed, but it's meaning and teachings are still as solid as ever."

"The Church I've devoted my life to has lied to me?"

Sensing an opportunity to inflame her rage, Sloane pressed the issue, "yes, they lied, of course they lied. The Church was created to control the people of Gilgannon... you think they wouldn't lie to you?"

Dawn gripped the rope that tethered her hands together at either end, hands merely inches apart, and pulled at it; this was the only way for her to express her anger without furthering the tension by the rope that bound the knife to her chest. Her jaw ached as she gritted her teeth.

"There's value in the Book, regardless of how *real* it is," Sloane said.

"I'm not going to become an Inauron," Dawn muttered.

"Of course you are… you all will."

She let that comment weigh on Dawn, and Sloane sat back with self-satisfaction.

Dawn tried in vain to ground herself. She looked for ways to direct her attention. She saw that she was held near a campsite; three canvas tents had been erected, and a small fire burned nearby tended to by another Brother. Above her was the canvas awning from another, fourth, tent, this one was off to the side. The three around the campfire all faced inwards, creating a gathering point at the centre, but her tent was a few meters way, facing off to the side. Why wasn't she kept close to the centre? A few more Brothers were pacing the camp; there were four out there; that meant six in total, including Brother Sloane, and Brother Yuri, who was nowhere to be seen.

Her eyes flittered to the sky above. It was darkening; the few clouds she could see through the silhouetted mesh of branches took on a pinkish hue. It would soon be dark, and the campsite at the centre of the three tents would be the only light for miles. She dreaded the approach of the cold, dark night.

"Why isn't Addison with you?" Brother Sloane said, snapping Dawn's attention back to then interrogation. Dawn's eyes widened at the mention of his name. "Aren't you betrothed?"

"How do you know that?" It seems the Brothers at Penny Grove had learned *everything* about them from their families; assuming Brother Yuri was telling the truth.

"At this point, it'll be safer if you just assume we know everything. It'll prevent us from having to answer this question over and over."

Dawn kept her lips sealed, Addison is someone who she wouldn't talk about. She instead looked at the other Brothers, and noticed that they were doing everything they could not to meet her eyes.

She attempted to redirect Sloane again, "why aren't they looking at me, the other Brothers?"

"They're devout, and you're an Abomination."

"Then why are you here talking to me?"

"You killed Cillian, so it's my job to make you suffer."

"I'm not suffering." Even before the comment

left her lips, she knew that it was a mistake. In her mind, the best-case scenario of that outburst is that Sloane becomes more aggressive; she didn't even want to consider what the worst case might be.

"Did you kill Addison like you killed my brother?"

She tensed up once more, the blade across her chest rose a few millimetres closer to her neck.

"I hear Addison was a marriage of business orchestrated by your father. Do you even love Addison or are you just doing this out of obligation to your family?"

Dawn refused to answer the question.

"Did you kill him because it was easier than disappointing your father?"

"I didn't kill him," she exclaimed, the knife rising a little once more.

"Well, we haven't been able to detect him throughout these woods. Which means he's dead, or gone somewhere else, which is unlikely."

She frowned.

"We've detected most of the others; Lawson, Wendy, Stokely and Piper are just a few short miles away on the other side of the river... Corin is missing, much like Addison, and your friends Fleta and Kenley are not far away from here, probably trying to find a way to free you," she paused, surveying how Dawn responded to each name. "Bronson is with Brother Yuri."

She gulped, concern rising in her mind; Bronson with Yuri didn't sound good. Yuri was deceptive, and Bronson impulsive and impressionable. She needed to learn more, but she didn't want Sloane to learn how she feels about Bronson, else she'd press that button in her interrogation. "What's Brother Yuri doing with Bronson?"

Sloane smiled but refused to elaborate instead continuing her line of questioning, "we can't find Addison or Corin. Do you think they've left together? Happy for you to die whilst they survive?"

The thought made her sick to her stomach, a jealousy that she didn't know existed. She knew of no moment of attraction that Addison had ever expressed toward Corin, but that didn't stop the feeling of jealousy from bubbling up within her.

"You're here, awaiting a long, painful death, and your husband-to-be has just up and started a new life elsewhere with a rival of yours from the Sanctuary."

"No, that's not possible."

"Of course it's possible."

She felt the knife as it touched her throat, the cold sharp metal almost tickled as it lightly grazed her throat. She took a deep breath and closed her eyes.

"I'm sure by now you realise the gravity of your situation," Brother Sloane said, smirking. "I was permitted to toy with you, but Brother Yuri has instructed me to keep you alive. So, thanks to Brother Yuri, you've been saved from death. However, those thoughts of your beloved Addison fucking Corin will soon pervade your thoughts, and if you die when I'm not sitting right here, then it's not my fault."

At that, she stood, brushed her rear of the detritus from the mossy log, re-hooded herself and walked towards the camp.

Sloane was right, and Dawn cursed her own predisposition to jealousy. Thoughts of Addison and Corin started beating upon her as she tried to breathe away the rising feelings. She didn't want to believe Sloane, but alas, Addison had not returned after their fight. If he was currently in the arms of Corin, she knew it was all her fault.

She's the one that had struck Addison, she's the one that forced them apart, it was all her fault. It was her anger that had caused it all. Now, if Sloane was to be believed, Kenley and Fleta were going to try and rescue her, and she was certain they'd be captured as well. Their impending deaths were also her fault. Tears collected at the corners of her eyes, and she lamented her capture, her argument with Addison, and what she was certain would happen to her friends.

Whilst the tears trickled down her cheeks, a trickle of something else took her attention... the knife had pierced her skin, and from the wound, a thin rivulet of blood had emerged.

23

Tempered

Kenley hadn't realised that Fleta still held his hand, but became painfully aware the moment she tore herself free of him.

"What do you mean, he joined them?"

She was tense, reactionary.

"I saw little, but he cut a deal to spare you by joining them." Kenley's eyes were wide, still reeling from his vision.

"That stupid, idiotic, bastard!"

He'd never heard such vitriol from her, but her face reddened as she cursed. She meant it with her whole heart.

Kenley was silent; a painful realisation had just crept upon him, and he struggled to find an explanation that made sense. Fleta, unaware of

Kenley's retreat, continued to rage.

"A stupid decision! How dare he take my own choices away from me!" She was unstoppable. "After what he'd heard about our... Our fucking Uncle earlier, I thought he'd realise a bit more keenly how much I just want to own my own decisions and own my life."

The tears flowed freely from her deep-set eyes.

"He couldn't even get the first thing right; I don't care if my decisions are successful, I just want to be able to make them. How dare he do this on my behalf!"

She locked eyes with Kenley whose chin trembled.

"Say something," she yelled.

He couldn't.

"What is it," she demanded.

He struggled with his words, stumbling over them clumsily. "If he's made a deal to spare you, it means that the rest of us are... what? Going to be killed?"

"Oh... Inauron, no," Fleta slumped. "I couldn't get my stupid mind off of my own stupid situation, I hadn't even realised."

"You're not stupid," he timidly let out.

Her head tilted to the side and her curious eyes told him she thought he was lying to her.

"I'm serious," his matter-of-fact tone drove the point home. "At the end of all this, I know you'll be able to make a life for yourself somewhere special."

"You're not going to die," she said. "I won't let that happen. We have to stop Bronson."

"What can *we* do?" Kenley said. "I may randomly blackout and have a vision, and then I'll be a liability to any rescue effort. We should probably just find a way to hide and leave forever."

"I told you, I won't let that happen," Fleta said, with a determination and fire burning within her heart.

He felt uneasy, scared-even. Since they left the safety of the Grove, they'd been constantly in danger; he wanted it to end. Saving Dawn and Bronson seemed to be a route to extend the misery they all felt, to continue the danger. Kenley saw it as a snowball rolling downhill, every new act only increased the size and strength of the danger, every step mattered, and the danger would only grow. He wanted to step out of its path instead.

There was another reason that Kenley wanted to avoid conflict, a reason that somehow furthered his lack of courage. Bronson's deal wasn't all he saw in his premonition, and when thought back to that vision of Fleta lying there on the wooden floor, atop a threadbare rug, blood leaking from a wound in her stomach staining the fabric beneath her; it made him nauseous. He felt things for Fleta that he hadn't previously allowed himself to acknowledge, and this sense of kinship he had with her wanted him to fight as hard as he could against the inevitability of what he saw.

Could he even influence his vision? If he saw something, then altered his behaviour to account for it, then would it still come to pass? Or would his vision have already accounted for that change in behaviour? Was everything we saw a true prediction of events to come, or was it a warning to help him change his path?

He closed his eyes and saw it again, as clear as day, he was looking down upon her body, the life-force slipping away from her as two people rushed towards her - to help or to harm? He had no way of knowing.

"I want us to just leave this Inauron-forsaken place," he said, the nausea taking its toll upon him. "I want us to go north, to Orenide, or further, to find a farm we can work, or a place we can hunt. I want us to move away, forget about all of this, and just put it all behind us."

"How can you say that?" she said, frowning. "You'd leave Dawn to die? Leave Bronson to join a group that'll spend the rest of their days hunting you?"

The thing about his vision that really stuck

with him was the location - there were no wooden floors in this forest; she was in a house somewhere, maybe in Penny Grove, maybe elsewhere... but in the vision, she was wearing the same dark green gown that she had on right now. Is this a coincidence perhaps? Does the vision *actually* happen in the far future and she, just by happenstance, is wearing the same attire? Or does it happen at the conclusion of this inevitable conflict with these grey-cloaked men? His heart beat faster.

"It's not that I want to leave them to die," he said sheepishly.

"You're just, what? Trying to save yourself?" she said.

"No," he said sternly. "This is not about me."

"Then why are you trying to leave? Why are you trying to back away from our plan to rescue Dawn and save my brother?" she was getting more heated. "Make me understand."

Kenley stood, ran his fingers through his curly dark hair and paced back and forth. Fleta sat, allowing him to vent his frustration hoping she'd finally break through his cowardice.

"It's not me," he said. "I don't care about me. I don't care what happens to me... no that's not right... I care what happens to me, but my life isn't what's giving me pause."

"Then what is it?"

"It's you," he said quietly, then fell to his knees, tears welling up in his eyes.

Fleta tightened her lips and looked to the floor. Instinctively, she knew he'd seen something in his vision.

"What did you see?"

"It doesn't matter what I saw," he said. "What matters is how I try to fix it."

"I'm not going to let you leave here without telling me," she said gritting her teeth. "If you've seen something, then you need to tell me, especially if it means I may walk into a trap. If you don't tell me, you're killing me."

Where had her determination come from? She had a strength of will he'd never seen from her, and it made him bristle; he wanted to see her succeed, develop, grow, blossom… but he feared telling her would only hasten the inevitable.

She moved closer to him, took his hands in hers and looked into his eyes.

"Tell me everything," she said.

And so he let the words flow. He told her how he saw her on the ground, atop the blood-soaked rug, with the wooden floor beneath, as the light seemed to fade from her eyes. He told her of the two faceless people that rushed to her side, about how he was unsure whether those people were her assailants or were rushing to her aid. The whole time he spoke, she nodded, squeezed his hands to comfort him. It was like he was telling her about a book he'd read, or a play he'd seen performed at The Sanctuary - she took the knowledge in her stride, never wavering from her goal. Why wasn't she shocked at what he'd seen?

When he was done, she tilted her head quizzically as she regarded him.

"Looks like whatever happens to me doesn't happen here, in the Wildlands," she said. "There are no houses out here. What did the rug look like?"

He took a breath, still reeling from the retelling, "like it was made from potato sacks, but had a green pattern painted upon it."

She nodded as he said it, recognising it, "it's at my house."

Then she stood, and it was her turn to pace back and forth in front of him.

"Do you know what this means?" she said excitedly. Kenley opened his mouth, but had no answer for her. "It means that we go home."

She smiled, as if a weight had been lifted from her, "I'm certain that you saw my parents coming to my aid, and it was in my house."

He took a breath, feeling the easing of tension as she became accustomed to her fate - though Kenley worried she was learning the wrong lesson from his vision. Instead of focusing on her dying body, she focused on the house.

"We're a long way from Penny Grove," she said. "So whatever happens with Dawn and Bronson, happens way in the future. This means that they don't kill me today - either Bronson's deal saves my life, or we win, but either way, I'm going to be safe."

"Hold on," Kenley said. "I don't know enough about these visions to tell you for certain you'll be safe. I don't know if they show the absolute future, or just a *possible* future."

"Everything you've seen so far has come to pass," she said. She sounded almost excited; Kenley worried his revelation would make her reckless, which could put her in even more danger than before. He could see the passion behind her eyes, and he knew already that there was nothing he could do to stop her.

"I don't want you to get hurt," he said quietly. "The vision may be where you die, but that doesn't mean that these grey-robed people can't hurt you - you don't know the fate of Dawn, or your brother, or me."

She slowed, then kneeled down to face him.

"You said some really important things earlier, about how I always put others before myself. I know that to be true, and whilst I'll try to help everyone, I know I can't make myself *responsible* for everyone," she said. "All I can do is try my best to save the people I love."

The Fleta of before would tie herself in knots at the prospect of putting others in harm's way, but this Fleta that sat before him had a confidence and resolve that would give her the energy to push through any hardship she experienced. She'd had such a great leap forward in her character that he felt a sense of pride, despite him having no part in her blossoming.

"I'd be willing to put myself in harm's way, to test this little 'deal' of Bronson's, if I thought it would help keep everyone safe. I don't need to wrap myself up in cotton wool any more, I can survive this," she said, stroking Kenley's face gently.

"Let me wrap you in cotton wool, then," Kenley said, "let me look out for you, let me focus on keeping you safe. I want to do that."

"Your idea of keeping me safe is to keep me far away," she said. "…and if I let you do that, then our lives would never be what we want them to be."

Kenley felt a sickness rise in his stomach; he needed to tell her how he felt about her, for he feared this was his last opportunity to do so… but his body and mind resisted him speaking. His anxieties rose, and his cheeks flushed, in anticipation of his embarrassment and inevitable rejection, but this was his only opportunity. He would regret it his whole life if he let this moment slip away.

"I want to keep you safe, Fleta," he said, breathing heavily, "because I... I'm..."

"Kenley," she said, stopping him. "I know what you're about to say."

"Then let me say it," he said. He took a long, determined breath in, and then he let it out. "I love you."

He studied her expression; her eyebrows lifted at the centre, and her lips parted slightly. In the painful pause, he reminded himself of her past trauma, and he felt shame wash over him. *She doesn't need this. She shouldn't have to hear this from someone she trusts.*

Suddenly, she opened her arms and hugged him tightly. Her warm embrace melted him, and he closed his eyes as he caught her scent.

She whispered in his ear, slowly, methodically, "I want to say the same for you..."

His heart caught in his throat, and his extremities chilled.

"... I care about you, Kenley. More than I've ever cared for another person..."

He wrapped his arms around her, holding their bodies close.

"... but I just don't know what that means."

"I understand," he whispered back.

"I want to say it back, but I think I need to first learn what it is I'm saying, and what that means for me," she said, apologetically. "So much of my life has been dictated for me, that I've never been able to learn about what I want, or even how I'm supposed to feel. My emotions have never been mine to command."

He closed his eyes, relishing this closeness.

"I don't know how I should feel, or what I should say, or what I should do," she said, "and until I feel safe, I just can't spend the time to learn."

"You don't need to say it back," Kenley assured her. "Before you run headlong into danger, you just need to know that there are some people out here who love you."

She held him tighter, burying her head into his shoulder and neck.

"I need nothing back from you," he said. "I just wanted you to know how I felt."

She pulled back from the hug and looked into his eyes; hers were glassy, but beautiful. Then she kissed him. It was just a peck on the lips... but it was a peck he would remember for the rest of his life. Her lips were cold from the forest air, but so were his, and he closed his eyes as he savoured the feeling.

"I want to find out about my feelings," she said. "I just need all this to be over before I can do that. But… thank you, it means a lot that I've got someone out here who has my back."

"Always," he said.

24

A Necessary Distraction

Bronson entered the campsite with Brother Yuri; his head freshly shorn, with a grey cloak wrapped around his body. He bore the stain of ash upon his forehead, from Yuri's short induction ceremony. He was now a Brother of Inauron; a member of a militant, zealous sect. He was now charged with hunting all the people across Gilgannon who were just like him.

His heart bore a scar that he didn't think he'd ever be able to heal. He was about to watch his friends be killed; every single one of them, but he did it all to keep Fleta safe. He'd failed as a brother, letting her be present at the fire, letting her spirit die as Brother Yuri told him. Devoting his life to keeping her safe was the only penance he felt as though he deserved. Even if this 'husk' was no longer the Fleta he knew, he still wanted her, safe from harm.

The glow had now faded fully from the sky above, leaving the campfire the only source of light in the campsite. The flickering orange illuminated the tents, the woodpile, and the faces of all the Brothers.

Bronson held his head down, looking at his feet, nervous, scared, but feeling confident in his decision.

"Brothers," Yuri announced, "gather around."

The five Brothers in the camp moved closer, standing in a semi-circle around him, looking him up and down, inspecting him like he was a piece of meat.

"I'd like everyone to welcome Brother Bronson to the order," Yuri said. "He bears our gift, and I see in him a lot of potential."

"Welcome, Brother Bronson," they said in unison. Yuri held out a small plate of ash that he used to anoint Bronson's shorn head before they entered. Each Brother, in turn, placed a thumb in the ash and placed it on Bronson's forehead. As each thumb lay in contact with Bronson, they introduced themselves.

"I'm Brother Ezekiel," said a thin, dark-skinned man who looked to be around forty. "Welcome, Brother."

"I'm Brother Sloane," said a hulking woman who wore a sneer of anger upon her face.

"Welcome, Brother."

"I'm Brother Kallan," said a stocky, short man, with skin whiter than anyone else Bronson had seen. "Welcome, Brother."

"I'm Brother Petyr," said the next, a heavily accented, tanned-skinned, tall man, who looked only a year older than Bronson. "Welcome, Brother."

"I'm Brother Laine," said a middle-aged man, who had the harsh lines across his face that Bronson recognised as someone who works the fields. "Welcome, Brother."

"Thank you," Bronson said quietly, he hunched, meekly, attempting in vain to avoid the scrutiny of his new family. As they each took time with him, he kept his sister close in his thoughts; he wondered how he looked to her now, fully bald, with ash across his head, wearing the garments of their enemies. He just needed to keep her safe.

"Brother Bronson has joined us on the condition that we spare his sister," Yuri said. "I trust you all know what to do here, when the opportunity arrives."

They all nodded together, silently.

"Take a seat around the fire," Yuri offered him. "We're going to share with you some of our order's history."

He complied, taking a seat on a flat rock,

hopefully not stealing anyone else's position. He pulled awkwardly at his grey robe as it folded uncomfortably below his rear. The other Brothers corralled around, taking their places opposite and beside him as they encircled the blaze.

"The first, and most important thing you need to be aware of," Brother Yuri started, "is that Inauron did not exist."

Bronson's eyes widened.

"Now, before you get all indignant, there did in-fact exist a person who did all the things that Inauron did, but Inauron isn't his name; his real name is lost to history."

Brother Sloane added, "what we are all afflicted with, is an Aura. We are called Aurons. Before the founding of The Church, Aurons ruled Gilgannon, and nearly every single thing they did caused immense strife and hardship for the people of the world. It was a tiered civilisation; if you were lucky to be born with the disposition to take upon an Aura, you were a part of the elite, otherwise you were forced to endure hardship for the gain of the Aurons. There were countless wars, famine, death on every corner, all at the whims of these afflicted Abominations we call Aurons."

Young Brother Petyr picked up from where Sloane left off, "The Inauron, the first one, was one such Auron, and he was one of the first to recognise the corrupting influence of the Aura itself. He vowed to rid himself of his Aura, and in doing so, he created a movement within the people. What started with his simple sacrifice, lit a fire beneath the people who were tired of being subjugated by the petty, angry and callous Aurons who ruled the world. The Church of Inauron was born from the ashes of the subsequent war, and since then its teachings have been entirely devoted to the elimination of those problematic traits that caused the prior regime. For over eight hundred years, The Church of Inauron has kept the world fed, safe, calm and happy."

Bronson struggled to understand what they were saying to him; The Book of Inauron seemed only a fairy-tale version of the story they told. He felt nausea in his stomach as he comprehended the lies he'd grown up believing.

"So what about The Book?" he asked.

"Across the centuries of rule, the Church of Inauron has adapted and rewritten the Book, reinterpreting its message with each generation," Brother Kallan said, "now, it bears little resemblance to the actual events of the past. The Book of Inauron has never been taught as a historic document, only as a series of life lessons and morals to live by."

"Why have I never heard about Aurons, or Aura, before? What about Abominations?" he gulped as he realised that the very presence of his gift made him an Abomination by the standards of The Book. "This has to do with The Sanctuary tree?"

"As I said before," Yuri jumped in, "the tree is a ward that keeps the entire town safe from affliction. Aurons are a disease that needs to be excised quickly else they destabilise the world. When the tree was damaged, you became afflicted. Yes, that means you are an Abomination."

"Brother Bronson," Laine said, "your life isn't over now that you're considered an Abomination. Our order will keep your curse in check, and following our rules will allow you to overcome any residual effects that the Aura thrusts upon you."

Residual effects? Corrupting Aura? Bronson felt light-headed; the foundations that he'd built his entire worldview upon were collapsing right in front of him.

"What's going to happen to me?"

"If you follow our teachings," Brother Laine continued, "then you'll thrive. If not, then you'll succumb to the affliction and will share the fate of any other Abominations we see on our path. Y'see, our order, The Brothers of Inauron, are the Church's failsafe against Auric uprising. If Aurons are permitted to exist, then their powers and strength can easily overpower and subjugate the world, as they did in ages past. Just look at what your friend Dawn did to four of our best. Imagine that, on a world-level scale."

Bronson gulped. "Where is she?"

"Don't worry about Dawn," Yuri said, "she's still alive, safe and contained."

Bronson couldn't help himself looking around the camp to see if he could see her. He spied a tent, separated from the rest, but in the night's dark, he could barely make out any details.

"Do you understand now why we exist?" Yuri asked.

He thought for a moment, closing his eyes whilst he considered his words, then he nodded slowly.

"We may act the aggressor," Yuri said, "but we're trying to keep the world safe. It's the most important charge anyone can have in this society; we are the silent heroes, working from the shadows to keep the world from spiralling out of control."

"Is everyone in Penny Grove going to die?"

"Yes," said a voice from behind them.

It was Fleta.

The Brothers all stood sharply and turned to face her.

"We saw it happen," she said. Bronson's shock

at her appearance rendered him silent. Why was she here? She was going to ruin everything.

"Ahh…" Yuri said, smirking as he turned to face her, "looks like we have a Voyauron to contend with… but I can see it's not you, dear. I take it Kenley is the one with the sight?"

"Bronson, leave here, come with us," she said, ignoring the others.

"You've not awakened yet," Yuri said, "which makes you a bit of a mystery."

"Bronson, let's go," she said.

The Brothers began to stand and walk towards the side of the camp that Fleta emerged from; Bronson stood and followed, concern etched across his brow.

"It's odd to have a grouping of more than two different Aura in a single community," Yuri continued, "normally groups of people in these small towns are so homogenous in temperament that everyone seems to develop the same set of afflictions. So… if I was a betting man, I'd say you're either linked with your Brother's, Kenley's, or dear Dawn's. The latter presents a much larger problem for us than we realised. Tell me… are you an angry person?"

"Fleta, get out of here," Bronson spat, weaving between the canvas tents to approach her.

"We'll sort this out eventually, I'm sure," Yuri

said, as he continued to orate despite being ignored.

"I'm here to keep you safe," Bronson continued, arguing through gritted teeth. "Get out of here."

"What about our family?" she asked. "You gonna kill them yourself? Is this what you want from your life?"

Bronson was seeing the wisdom in Yuri's judgement earlier at the decoy camp; Fleta was different, ruined... afflicted. There's no way that his little Flea would ever stand and confront a group like this, especially when it puts her at risk of harm; his Flea was meek, quiet and child-like. This Fleta, whoever she was now, was unruly, fearless, and foolhardy.

Yuri stopped talking and stood smugly, watching as the two twins battled it out with their words.

"Everyone's already dead," he yelled at her. "Everyone died the moment the Sanctuary burned."

Yuri locked eyes with Brother Kallan and spoke within his mind, Bronson could hear every word with the gift he shared with them.

"Check on our little guest," Yuri said. "The other one might be lurking around... you never can be too careful."

Kallan moved quickly toward Dawn's tent,

disappearing from Bronson's sight.

"I'm not dead, and I will not die either," she said, resolutely. The Brothers stood back, smiling, watching the exchange as if they were enjoying an entertaining stage-play. This was their opportunity to see if Bronson would do what needed to be done, or at least whether or not their teachings had stuck.

"Everyone's dead, including me," Bronson said. "All that's left is to clean up the mess we made."

"Is that what I am to you?" she said, folding her arms. "A mess?"

"No... I," he stammered, unable to bring himself to say it. "You're different. You're broken."

"I am broken," Fleta said, "but now, I'm finally feeling that I'm not a lost cause; for the first time in Inauron-knows how long, I'm feeling free."

"Sadly, that freedom you feel does not extend to the lives of all those you hold dear," Brother Yuri said.

A scream rang out from the direction of Dawn's tent, as human viscera erupted from behind the trees.

25

The Bold and Brave

Kenley snuck through the bushes, being mindful of every step. He thought of his father's hunting books as he crept, imagining the Brothers as prey he was encircling. He gingerly stepped over sticks, ensuring his footing was perfect before shifting his weight, careful that his passing didn't disturb the foliage.

He peeked between the trees, and saw Dawn, laying face-first on the ground beneath a canvas awning. He craned his neck one way, then the other, before stepping forward in front of her tent. The moonlight above provided the most miniscule semblance of light that pierced the canopy overhead; the shadows beneath were long and all-encompassing.

He neared Dawn, and she sensed his footing

around her, bristling when she felt him. She looked up, then her eyes widened when she realised it was Kenley. She'd abandoned all hope of being found, but even then, she didn't seem eager to see him. Kenley frowned and leaned in close to her ear.

"I'm getting you out of here," he said.

"Why?"

"What do you mean, 'why'?" he said, furrowing his brow. "I'm saving your life."

"My life's not worth saving," Dawn said flatly.

"Oh, Inauron, what did they do to you?" Kenley asked.

"All of this pain and suffering is my fault; let me die here," she said.

"You think it's just you?"

She looked over at him, barely able to see his expression beneath the dark canopy.

"Fleta's about to do something stupid, and you need to fucking save her," he said. "We know what you can do, we saw what you did to those Brothers, and now we need you to do it again to save Fleta."

"I can't," she said, emotionlessly, blank. "I've hurt everyone around me, and I don't want to do that again."

"Okay," he said, turning away from her. "Leave Fleta and Bronson to die, see if that makes you feel any better about yourself."

She gritted her teeth, then exhaled loudly, "wait."

"That's what I thought," he said, pulling the knife that Brother Yuri had left in the tree from his belt. "Now tell me how to undo this spider's web of ropes."

"There's a knife at my chest," she said. "If I pull on these ropes, the knife will kill me."

Kenley gulped, and then lifted Dawn's body so she sat upon her knees. There he saw the knife and noticed the blood that stained her neck, chest, and the front of her clothing; it was disguised well by the maroon fabric of her gown, but the moonlight had caught the wetness of it.

"Inauron!" he exclaimed, seeing the tip of the knife as it pressed into a small puncture wound at her neck. "Let me see how to get this off."

He looked her over closely, scanning and tracing each rope until he could understand how the binding worked. Then he focused on the ropes that tied the knife in place.

"In theory," he said, "If I cut through this rope here at the knife's hilt, I should be able to pull it downwards and remove it from the binding."

"Check it again," Dawn said, gulping. Kenley nodded, accepting the risk of his task on Dawn's life.

"Got it," he said, then started cutting

through the rope at the knife's hilt. He gently slid the knife downwards, and out from the rope, releasing it from her body. She let out an exhausted, relieving breath; finally free of the knife. The ropes still bound her tight, and Kenley's cut had evidently only severed a supplemental piece of the binding. She was no less bound than before, but she at least was out of the danger posed by her temper.

"Everyone's already dead," they heard Bronson yell. Kenley, alarmed by the volume, instinctively stepped backwards, towards the thicket opposite her.

"Hide," Dawn mouthed to Kenley as she saw one of the Brothers approaching her. She fell forward once more, placing her head back into the dirt, hiding the place at her chest where the knife had been. Kenley stepped back behind a bush and shrunk down as deeply as his body would allow.

One of the Brothers who had earlier avoided eye contact looked her up and down, inspecting her bindings. She lay on her front, preventing him from seeing the severed rope. He walked around the canvas tent, wary of the possibility of Kenley's appearance, before he circled back around, standing directly in front of Dawn.

"Won't be long until you're no longer needed," he spat quietly.

"When I get out of these ropes, I'm going to

tear you apart," Dawn said, her forehead pressed into the mud.

He squatted down in front of her, "you're not getting out of these ropes, Abomination. You'll die in them."

She gritted her teeth and pulled at the rope.

"That's right, hasten the inevitable," he said, unaware of the knife's removal.

Kenley's heart pounded as he watched the exchange.

He needed to do something; he wasn't sure how Dawn's strength worked, or if it would even allow her to tear herself free. His ability was seemingly random, and if Dawn's was too, then she was stuck there for the time being. He considered his options, Fleta, his love, was exposed to the danger of the Brothers, and the only person who could save her was stuck in the mud in front of him. He gulped. Only he could free her, only he could fix this. Time was passing, and every new moment without rescue left Fleta even more in danger. He needed to get rid of this Brother.

He held one knife in his hand tightly and tucked the one coated in Dawn's essence into his waistband. Then he took a breath, before he leapt from the bush. He jumped up, landing upon Brother Kallan's back, wrapping a hand around his mouth to keep him from yelling out. Then, with his other hand, stabbed the knife deep into his neck, causing the man to fall to his knees.

Dawn pulled hard at the rope, trying her best to access the strength she so feared.

She felt them give, and they finally tore apart. Kenley fell backwards, still holding the Brother across the mouth, with the knife buried in his neck. Dawn approached, anger scarring her expression. She grabbed the wounded Brother by the scruff of his neck and by the belt at his waist and lifted him above her head. Blood flowed from the open wound in his neck, coating the ground as she held him aloft. His scream started the moment Kenley's hand left his mouth. As her rage reached its apex, she pulled his body apart, with all her might. She grimaced through her strain, separating his body at the middle, tearing him across his stomach. She threw the pieces of him forward and as his gore misted in the air.

Then, she began a fiery stomp towards the campsite.

✽ ✽ ✽

"She's free!" Brother Yuri bellowed.

Pieces of Brother Kallan landed near them; Brother Yuri yelled out an instruction, and Sloane, knowing what she had to do, took off to lead Dawn away from them.

"Come get me," Sloane said. "You'd better not forget about me, because if you do, I'm going to take great pleasure killing your betrothed."

Dawn couldn't contain her ire, and she, like a bull, centred all her anger at Brother Sloane. She altered her direction and instead of heading towards the campsite; she focused all her energy on her target. Brother Sloane took off quickly into the darkness of the forest, and Dawn charged after her.

Despite her mountainous form, Brother Sloane moved swiftly through the trees. Dawn struggled to keep pace, but the only thought dominating her psyche was the desperation to kill Sloane, to tear her limb from limb, to bathe in her blood.

Is this what her anger brought her to? Was she a natural-born killer or did this mysterious Aura do that to her?

Sloane turned, leapt over a fallen log, and disappeared behind some thick bushes. Dawn repeated her actions but found herself stood in a small clearing, alone. She could still see the blaze of the fire from the camp as a small glow in the distance, and she listened intently for any movement indicative of Sloane's whereabouts.

"You won't be able to save them, y'know," Sloane said, speaking directly into Dawn's head.

"Get out of my head," Dawn said.

"I told you, girl," the voice continued, "I'm not a fighter. I use words. And I'll use those words to make you destroy yourself."

Dawn paused, crouched and listened for any movement. Her rage was heating her body and her limbs felt tight from the adrenaline.

"Is it Addison you really want?" Sloane said. "Or, is it Brother Bronson?"

"Don't call him that," she spat. "He's no Brother to you."

"He took the rites," she argued. "He's a Brother, and there's nothing you can do about it. Your one true love has joined the ranks of your enemy."

Dawn lashed out, punching a nearby tree. A split snaked its way up the thick trunk, and one half of the enormous tree fell towards the ground, hitting branches of adjacent trees and breaking itself apart as it descended.

"Furaurons are weak, y'know," Sloane laughed. "Not in strength… but in ability. The advantage I have over you is that I may be meters away, or miles away, and you'll never know the difference. I can spend my life enraging you, taunting you, from the comfort of the capital, and there's nothing you can do about it."

Dawn took a breath, trying to steel herself. In the glimpse of clarity afforded by the breath, she realised Sloane would likely move back towards the campsite to help contend with and subdue Fleta, Kenley and Bronson - if, of course, Bronson had the wherewithal to snap out of his delusion. Sloane was probably sneaking back there right now, doubling back on herself. Dawn looked through the trees and saw the campfire's blaze in the distance. She stared, squatting to get a better view.

A shadow crossed in front, between Dawn and the fire… That had to be Sloane. It didn't take her long for her anger to climax once more, and she took off running to follow the distant figure.

Sloane had misjudged her; thought herself better than Dawn, but Dawn had spotted her, slinking low through the dense foliage. Brother Sloane was comfortable in the assumption that she'd won her battle of wits, but her confidence was about to fall apart.

"Got you," Dawn said, and Sloane span to face her.

Dawn bore her fingernails and with a single swipe downwards, she tore through Sloane's skin like it was butter, throwing her to the side. She screamed as she flew through the air.

"When I hit your brother in the face, it was the first time I had ever accessed this power," Dawn said, closing the gap between herself and Sloane's crumbled form. The mountainous woman mumbled something incoherently as she tried to scramble along the ground. "I hit him, and his head nearly left his body."

Sloane spat blood as Dawn stood over her weakening body. The open scars the claws left across Sloane's face had torn her flesh to pieces, her lip was flapping free with her breathing, and blood pooled amongst her teeth. Her eyeball looked damaged beyond repair, and her head fell loosely back and forth as she tried to maintain consciousness.

"The problem with how I killed your brother though," Dawn said, squatting to lean into Sloane. "It was too fast. He didn't experience any of the terror that you're currently experiencing."

"Fuck you," Sloane spat, blood sprayed at Dawn's face. "Abomination."

"I'm done, here," Dawn said, rising, before pulling Sloane's leg along with her. As Sloane struggled against Dawn, who dragged her easily through the undergrowth, to a space between the trees and away from the thick bushes. Gripping Sloane's leg tightly, Dawn pulled and span, throwing her wounded victim with all her might at the enormous tree in front of her. Sloane's body dismantled itself in a red mist with the impact.

Dawn gritted her teeth, then looked towards the campsite.

❊ ❊ ❊

"She's free!" Brother Yuri bellowed. Before Fleta could register what was happening, Sloane had run off, and Dawn, now free had given chase. Brother Laine made as if to join Sloane in her pursuit, but then at the last moment, turned and clasped an arm around Fleta's neck from behind. He held one arm around Fleta's neck, and bent the other arm upwards to lock his fist in place around her.

She struggled against his strength, but he was too much. She tried to kick out with her feet, or scratch at his face with her fingernails, but Laine deftly dodged all her attempts at freeing herself.

"Stop," Bronson shouted. "This wasn't the deal. You let her go."

Brother Laine looked into Bronson's eyes,

quizzically.

"We can't let an Auron go free," he said. "Don't be so childish."

Bronson's eyes shot to Yuri, who shrugged, then smirked.

"I'm sorry, boy," Yuri said. "What Brother Laine said is true... our deal was never enforceable."

"Then why agree to it?" Bronson spat.

"Well, because if you're here, then... Fleta would come to us," he said, then gestured to Fleta standing restrained before him. Bronson looked around. It was Fleta and he against Yuri, Petyr, Ezekiel and Laine; painfully outnumbered.

Bronson took a step towards his sister, but Ezekiel put a hand on his chest, and silently shook his head.

"Let it happen, Bronson, boy," Yuri said.

"No," he shouted, his eyes not leaving Ezekiel's. "Let her go."

"That will not happen," Yuri said. "We are going to kill her... but we're willing to let you keep your robes afterwards. You're a Brother just like us now; you share our mission."

"You're going to kill her right in front of me, and expect me to stay in the Order?" Bronson laughed. "If you touch her, I'm going to make it my life's mission to hunt you down and destroy you."

The four Brothers laughed.

"Not the first time we've heard threats like that," Ezekiel said, pushing Bronson a step backwards with his palm at Bronson's chest. "But if you decide to give up your place in the Order, then your life is just as forfeit as your sisters? It's not 'with us, or against us'... It's 'with us, or dead'."

"Push me again," Bronson said, challenging Ezekiel.

His assailant smiled, then pushed.

Bronson quickly grabbed at Ezekiel's fingers and twisted, snapping them. The Brother fell to the ground, screaming.

Yuri sighed, disappointed, then spoke to Petyr through his mind.

"Get the spears," he ordered. "Looks like we're going to have a battle."

Bronson looked around himself, the firelight illuminated far too little for his liking. As Petyr went left to get the weapons, Bronson went right, finding a small woodcutting hatchet in the dirt in front of the woodpile.

Fleta continued to jostle and struggle within Laine's arms, but the more she laboured, the higher Laine lifted his arms, and the less grip upon the floor she had.

Bronson returned to the camp with the hatchet, and pointed it at Laine, "you let my sister go."

"Why would I do that?" Laine said.

Petyr returned with two spears, he handed one to Yuri, and held the other, dropping himself into a combat pose, pointing the spearhead at Bronson.

He looked downwards, at Ezekiel, who crawled along the ground cradling his fingers. He stepped over him, with a foot either side and looked down.

"Let her go, or say goodbye to your Brother," he said, holding the hatchet above his head.

"Bronson, Bronson, Bronson," Yuri started in a manner far too calm for Bronson's liking. "Here's a thing we hadn't got around to teaching you yet... we're all so fervent and zealous in our desires for peace, that we're all prepared to die. We all came out here knowing that death was an option. You won't get anywhere by threatening our lives."

He gritted his teeth, then kicked at Ezekiel's prone body.

Bronson lifted the hatchet, looked towards Laine and considered whether he could throw it with any level of accuracy. He shook his head, not trusting his ability enough to protect his sister.

It was a stale-mate. He had no moves left to make and his hope was dwindling.

* * *

Kenley threw up in the bushes after seeing what Dawn had done to that Brother. He'd seen the results of her carnage before, but there was something deeply disturbing about seeing it in person. She tore him in half. He tried as fast as he could to compose himself enough to make his way to the campsite, but the nausea continued to overwhelm him.

He kept to the bushes, and crept through them, staying out of sight as much as possible until he stood close enough to see what was happening. Fleta was being choked from behind by one Brother, whilst two others held spears pointing at Bronson. A fourth Brother lay on the ground between Bronson's legs, holding an injured hand to his chest.

He saw the choker lift Fleta so high she struggled to kick against the ground; she would soon lose consciousness... Kenley had to do something. He pulled out both knives and stepped forward gingerly until he stood behind the Brother. He remembered his father's book, there was a way to quickly collapse any predator that could overwhelm you, and he looked at the man in front of him with an idea. In one quick movement, he slashed with both knives at the tendons behind the man's ankles, digging deep into them and slashing them free from the man's legs.

Laine emitted a bloodcurdling scream before falling backwards, pulling Fleta with him, collapsing on top of his bent ankles, snapping the bones as he fell. He landed atop Kenley, who caught the Brother before slicing at his neck finally loosening his grip upon Fleta.

As the sound of his scream rang out, Petyr looked backwards, and Bronson used the opportunity to throw the hatchet; it struck Petyr squarely in the side of his head, felling him instantly. Petyr tipped backwards, landing so the butt of the spear dug deep into the dirt. As he scrambled with his grip on the shaft, his body slid slowly on its way to meet the earth. He landed, still holding the spear, which was pointed outwards at an angle from his limp form; he was holding it up as if marking his grave.

Ezekiel kicked up too late to prevent Petyr's death, hitting Bronson between the legs. Bronson recoiled and fell backwards, coughing involuntarily. Yuri looked alarmed; it was the Brothers that were now outnumbered by the exiles.

Bronson crawled over to Ezekiel's body and began pounding upon him, overpowering the injured Brother who struggled to defend himself with his mangled hand. Bronson eventually struck him hard enough to watch the light fade from his eyes; for how long though, Bronson did not know. He then struggled to his feet, Kenley helped Fleta up, and the three stood in a semi-circle around Yuri.

With determination in his eyes, Yuri took up a fighting pose, lowering his body, pointing the spear towards them.

"Did you think I got to this age in our Order by cunning alone?" he spat. "For years I was the best fighter in the entire Order, and age has not dulled my senses."

Bronson walked across and pulled the hatchet from Petyr's head, then turned to face Yuri, joining the other two as they waited for Yuri's first move.

"You think a hatchet will help you?" he shouted, "you know nothing, boy."

Yuri's face contorted into a sneer, and he bellowed out, "you know nothing of the grace we offered you."

Kenley handed Fleta one of his blades, and

they shared a knowing glance.

Another scream rang out behind Yuri, beyond the treeline; Sloane.

Yuri looked to the side, and spat. The look in his eyes told Bronson all he needed to know - he knew Dawn would kill him, and that knowledge made him ever more dangerous. Yuri didn't need to worry about his own survival, he would now attack as recklessly as he could manage, taking as many of them down with him as he could.

"Well, I guess it's it for me," he said, "but it's not over yet."

He stepped forward and stabbed the spear towards Bronson. Bronson dodged the blow easily, and Fleta and Kenley repositioned themselves, in an attempt to flank their attacker. Yuri recovered from the miss quickly and his spear shot out behind himself unexpectedly, striking Kenley in the forehead with the weapon's butt. Kenley fell backwards to the ground, and then the assailant stabbed out with the spear again. The shock of seeing Kenley hit so unexpectedly allowed Yuri to bury the spear into Bronson's thigh, then, using his momentum, he pivoted on his foot, and kicked out with his other, striking Fleta in the chest.

Fleta fell backwards, tripping over Laine's fallen body, until the spear held by Petyr's corpse entered her lower back.

She gasped, but Bronson kept fighting Yuri whose assault was relentless. Petyr's spear had pierced Fleta's lower back and pushed through the front of her stomach beside her navel.

Time seemed to slow for Kenley as he dropped the knife he held and launched himself towards Fleta's wounded body. She slid down the spear a little way, and she held tight to the end that had passed through her, which was now slick with her blood.

"Bronson!" Kenley yelled, as he tried to hold Fleta's body up, preventing her from falling further. Bronson looked over, and his eyes widened. Seeing an opportunity, Yuri launched forward to stab a second time at Bronson; but before his spear could connect, Yuri's head left his shoulders.

Dawn had approached the carnage from behind, and in one quick movement, she swiped at Yuri's head; a swipe so strong, his body crumpled in place whilst his head bounced off the canvas tent and landed between Ezekiel's unconscious feet.

They had won; but their victory was meaningless.

Fleta spat blood as Bronson and Kenley tried to hold her body up, to prevent her from sliding further down the spear.

"What do we do? What do we do?" Kenley

cried.

Bronson gritted his teeth, as the emotional toll of what he was seeing weakened his limbs.

"Help me," Fleta gasped.

Suddenly, an incredible light emerged from Fleta's body, originating at her heart, it enraptured the group of them entirely, bathing them in light, blinding them. Kenley and Bronson felt Fleta's weight diminish until they felt as though they held nothing at all.

Then, as suddenly as it had arrived, the light dissipated, and Fleta was no longer upon the spear.

She was gone.

26

Gone

Kenley fell to his knees, and tears flowed.

"Where did she go?" Bronson said angrily, pacing back and forth. "Where the fuck did she go?"

Dawn's mouth stood agape; she'd just watched her friend vanish into nothingness.

"She just disappeared!" Bronson said. "Where is she?"

He stormed around the small campsite, looking in the tents, looking beyond the treeline, scanning around, not believing what his eyes had told him, limping as he moved from the wound in his leg.

He looked over at Kenley, who wept openly, and Bronson tensed his entire body, struggling to contain the rising emotions within him.

"What did you do?" he screamed at Kenley, before launching himself towards the boy, "what the fuck did you do to her?"

"What do you mean?" Kenley said, voice shaking. "I didn't do anything; I was trying to help her."

Bronson breathed angrily through his nose as he pressed his lips tightly together and gritted his teeth. He reached out, grabbing hold of Kenley by the front of his shirt and baring down upon him with his rage.

He threw Kenley to the ground, and jumped atop him, straddling the boy's body. Bronson placed his hands around Kenley's throat and squeezed.

"She fucking trusted you, and you let her die," he spat.

Dawn shook free of the shock of what she'd seen, and her mind took her a moment to catch up with what had happened since Fleta's disappearance; it was as if her mind was replaying the events she'd just witnessed in slow motion, whilst simultaneously refusing to believe it.

Bronson continued to squeeze Kenley's neck, shaking him, putting all the pressure of his body upon the boy.

"You were supposed to take her away," he screamed, "but you brought her right to them.

You killed her because you didn't take her away. You didn't protect her, you killed her."

Dawn finally realised what was happening, and her attention snapped to Bronson's assault. At once, she threw herself at him, pushing him away from the boy with far too much of her innate strength. Bronson's body took to the air then slid across the ground, hitting the gnarled roots of a nearby tree.

Kenley coughed violently, blood seeped from his eyeballs, and he struggled to regain his breath.

"You fucking killed her," Bronson screamed whilst holding his ribs as he fell back against the tree.

"*You* killed her," Dawn spat back at him, baring her teeth, "you fucking joined them."

Kenley continued to cough and Dawn rubbed his back to help him regain his composure. Blood streamed from the corners of his eyeballs down his face.

Bronson was silent.

"I can't see," Kenley whimpered. "I can't see anything."

Kenley convulsed; his whole body shook and blood spilled from his mouth, his nose, his eyes and his ears. He looked up at Dawn; terror gripped him, before his eyeballs turned a milky white, entirely. He fell limp.

"Kenley?" Dawn said, shaking him, but he gave no response.

"Leave him," Bronson said.

"I can't," Dawn said, panic rising in her voice.

"He'll snap out of it," Bronson barked. "It's his thing. He's seeing something."

"What do you mean?"

"A vision."

Dawn looked back at Kenley who lay silently. She wiped the Brothers' blood from her face as she waited.

"I hope, this time, he never comes back," Bronson said, rolling up to his knees.

"Why would you say that?"

"He killed Fleta," he said, flatly. "I'll never forgive him."

"You just don't get it do you?" Dawn snapped. "Kenley did everything right, he freed me, he saved Fleta, he *tried* to help you. He's the only one of us I can say for certain did everything right."

"When we split up, he was supposed to take her away," he said. "He didn't, and now she's gone."

"What's your role in this, then?" Dawn said. "You joined with the group that is actively hunting her, you called the one who actually killed her your Brothers. I can't even look at you, with your bald head and grey robes."

"This was the only way I could keep her safe," Bronson said, refusing to understand his role in Fleta's wounding.

"This is *all* on you," Dawn said, gritting her teeth. "It's all your fault. Don't you fucking dare blame anyone but yourself."

"I took a risk," he shouted, his volume rising and his gestures became more animated, "I know that. And everything would have worked out fine if Kenley had just kept her away."

"No," Dawn said, calmly. "I would be dead, Kenley would be dead, and they would use you to hunt down everyone else."

"But Fleta would live," he bellowed, spittle sprayed onto the ground with his passion. "I'll make it my life's mission to make sure Kenley pays dearly for this mistake."

"If you come near him," Dawn said angrily, "then I'll kill you myself. You're a selfish piece of shit; I can't believe I ever loved you."

"You never loved me," he said, his voice croaked as it returned to his normal speaking volume. "You only ever loved Addison."

"That's not true, and you know it," she said. "I had no choice with Addison - it was what my family wanted, and I, trusting my family's judgement, threw myself into the relationship like I was expected to. I *always* wanted you."

"Fucking someone else is a funny way of

showing it," Bronson spat, as he struggled to his feet.

"You just see the bad in everyone, don't you?" Dawn said. "Except the one person who matters... you. You criticise everyone else around, but everyone can plainly see how broken you are. I don't love *this* Bronson, I never could. The Bronson I loved was kind, caring, generous with his time, and always had a smile on his face. I don't even know who the fuck you are."

He leaned against the tree, reeling from the whole experience, unable to look Dawn in the eye. His eyes turned to the spear, still covered in Fleta's blood. He slid his body down against the trunk of the tree and eyed the spear wound in his thigh. In the silence that fell over the campsite, tears trickled down his face.

* * *

Kenley's mind flowed over events past, present and future, with no regard for chronology. He watched a horrifying, wrinkled crone spit blood in Corin's grey face; then a moment later, he watched his father deliver him from his mother. Then he saw

Wendy on her knees in front of Lawson in a small clearing in the trees as Lawson ran his fingers gently through her hair. Then he saw Addison in a pitch dark room, his face illuminated green by some sort of stone tablet, emitting a bright light, as he read through words that magically appeared upon its surface. Then he saw two wagon-loads of Brothers of Inauron as they passed through the gates of Penny Grove; the Sanctuary still smouldered in the distance - it must have been only moments since their banishment. Then, over to the rolling grassy plains between Penny Grove and Orenide Hills, as a group of assailants attacked the caravan of Brothers before being wiped out by the superior, battle-ready Brothers. Then he saw his father crying over his mother's body and he saw himself lying upon her cold body as a baby, cradled in her arms.

His mind span in circles, and he struggled to focus it - could he even sharpen his focus? Or, do the visions themselves decide what he sees? He wondered whether it was possible to influence what he was being shown... The pace and frequency of these visions this time fatigued him, and he desperately wanted to see what happened to Fleta. He just wanted to see her. He let the power of his volition flow through him as he attempted to picture her in his mind.

Suddenly he shifted and saw her standing

over Javi's broken and bloody corpse.

Not that... later.

He saw her at the clearing, dabbing a cold cloth over Bronson's forehead as he rode out the gravel withdrawal.

... Later.

He saw her as he did earlier that day, on the threadbare rug.

... Later.

"She's lost a lot of blood," Doctor Krilson said to Wentworth, Fleta's father. "I don't know how long she'll survive."

"You have to do something," Fleta's father pleaded.

"There's not much I can do," the Doctor said. "These Brothers are everywhere, and if they see me taking her to surgery, they'll kill me... and probably her too, and then maybe even come for you and Gracie. I'm sorry."

"Then, operate here," her father said. "What do you need?"

"Get me a fire poker, make it hot-hot," he said.

"We don't have one... The guards seized it after my brother..."

"Anything else iron you can heat?" the Doctor said, cutting him off.

"I've got some iron tools here that we could try," he said.

"Get them," the Doctor said.

... Later.

Fleta lay in her bed, bandaged, as the sun shone through the window.

Kenley swore he saw movement behind her eyelids, just a small amount... just enough. He focused and focused, pushing all his willpower into the vision, to see her closer, see whether or not she was alive.

Her eyes snapped open, and his vision dissipated, waking him up.

She was alive.

27

Aftermath

Kenley felt the cool night air enter his lungs as he gasped sharply; he coughed and spat as he tried to regain his consciousness. His eyesight hadn't returned, and so he began to panic. He felt around himself frantically until Dawn took his hand.

"What did you see?" she asked.

"I can't see anything," he said, a tremor hid within his voice. "I'm blind."

"Is Fleta alive?" Bronson shouted.

"What's happened? Where am I?" Kenley cried.

"You're with us, same as before," Dawn soothed. "How many fingers am I holding up?"

Kenley saw nothing, only blackness.

"I don't know..."

"Fuck that," Bronson said, throwing his arms up, then more pointedly he spoke to Kenley. "Is Fleta alive?"

"She's alive," he gasped. "I think she's alive."

Tears poured from his sightless eyeballs.

Bronson fell to his knees beside Dawn and placed his head in the dirt, as the emotion overcame him.

It was then that Brother Ezekiel stirred.

Almost immediately, Bronson was at his throat, screaming, "where is my sister?"

The Brother was confused, disorientated, Dawn could see that, but Bronson wasn't letting up, throwing fists into the man's ribs and threatening him. Bronson was going to kill him, and then they'd learn nothing. Dawn let go of Kenley's hand and stood to approach the conflict.

"Don't move," she said softly, to Kenley, "I'll be back."

"Wha... what do you mean?" Ezekiel yelled, his mind not yet fully his from the concussion.

Dawn put a hand on Bronson's shoulder, "let me."

He struggled to calm himself but he stepped off Ezekiel throwing him back to the ground.

"Fleta," Dawn started, squatting down over him. She tried her best to convey a safe and calm demeanour despite being covered in the

Brothers' blood and viscera. "She was injured, and then she disappeared."

"Disa… what?"

"Get it together," Dawn said, increasing her volume and narrowing her eyes. He knew what she was, he knew what she could do.

"Disappeared… umm… that probably means she's a Lociauron, they can go places…"

"What do you mean, places?"

"Anywhere they've been before, or anywhere they can see," he said, his eyes locked with Dawn's. "They think of it, and they go there."

"So where did she go?"

His mind was coming back to him now, and he was regaining his composure. "Why don't you ask Brother Bronson, he can speak to her."

"She's not fucking replying," Bronson shouted, punching a tree in frustration, before nursing his hand as regret seeped in.

"Then, I can't tell you either," Ezekiel said.

For the first time since he recovered, Ezekiel broke Dawn's penetrating glare to survey the campsite. The darkness made it difficult to work out what was happening and the glare from the blazing fire blinded him of any ability to adjust to the shadows. He could see blood splattered across the canvas tents, and felt something at his feet. He looked down to see Brother Yuri's head staring blankly up at him. He screamed and scrambled with his feet to move away from it.

"You're abominations... Monsters..." he said, whimpering as he tried in vain to tear his gaze away from Yuri's pale visage. "You've killed them all."

"Only the ones who tried to kill us," Dawn said.

"We *have to* kill you, it's our charge," he said, as the beginnings of tears assembled at the corners of his eyes.

"You've failed," Dawn said.

❊ ❊ ❊

"Are you sure about this?" Dawn asked, holding Kenley's arm as she led him through the woods. The early morning sun peered over the distant horizon as they neared the cliff's edge. The birds sang their song as they flittered between the branches.

"She's there, at home," he said. "Or, at least she will be."

"What do you mean?" Dawn said.

"I can't tell when the vision was, I don't know

if she opened her eyes after being asleep for a month, or if her eyes are already open. It happens when there's sunlight in her window, that's all I know."

"She's not responding to me," Bronson said, he trailed behind, filled with shame.

Kenley had told them where to go, and they all knew of the place - it was an outcrop that overlooked the village of Penny Grove. As they grew up, they always wanted to visit, but given that it was beyond the treeline in The Wildlands, they were always forbidden. The fables and mythology behind this place were more than sufficient to keep them out of the woods, even the most daring amongst them.

Together they had found the river and followed it back the way they came, but a few kilometres before they got to the town, they veered uphill, until they could see the outcrop, poking out of the elevated forest. Dawn guided Kenley as best as she could, given his blindness, she helped him over rocks, fallen trees and picked him up when he slipped or fell on unseen obstructions. It was tiring work, made even more difficult by the darkness of the night, and Bronson's wounded thigh. It had taken them until the sunrise to get to the cliff, and now the sun was rising in earnest.

"If she's being worked on by the doctor, she may not be able to reply," Kenley said.

"Watch the rock," Dawn said, tapping his leg as he struggled to step over. Kenley sight was gone, absolutely. He couldn't even perceive changes in light, which Dawn had witnessed when the sun first appeared and Kenley appeared to unblinkingly stare in its direction through the treeline. She would be his aide as long as was necessary; he had saved her life, and she owed him everything.

"Those Brothers weren't the only ones," Kenley said. "There's more in the Grove."

Dawn gasped, "why?"

"I assume to kill everyone," Kenley said. "I saw everyone being locked in the town hall whilst it burned."

"So then, why are we here, and not down there trying to help?" Bronson said.

Bronson had insisted on staying at the Brothers' campsite after Dawn had departed with Kenley towards the river. Bronson's eyes were dark, and there was a sadness bubbling up behind them. He'd said he needed to figure some things out and needed the quiet to do it. When he eventually caught up with them, he told them a tale of how he'd ended Ezekiel's life using one of the knives Kenley had wielded to cut his throat. All the rage and vitriol had now left Bronson's body, and he seemed cold, despondent and empty; a shell of himself.

"This is where we meet," Kenley replied.

"Who?"

"Everyone else," Kenley said. "We are the only ones who can rescue our families; only we can prevent the town from being wiped out."

Dawn furrowed her brow and tensed her arm upon his just as they passed the final group of trees. She looked out ahead of them at the few meters of scrub, grass and rocks until they reached the edge of the cliff. From where they stood, Dawn could see the beautiful landscape around Penny Grove, with the town itself nestled within the trees. At the town's centre, was the blackened husk of the Sanctuary; a blemish on an otherwise picturesque view. They were too high to see details, or people, or assess the situation with any level of accuracy.

"How long should we wait?" Dawn asked.

"Told you," Kenley replied flatly, "I don't know when my visions occur, only that they do."

"Right," she said.

She sat Kenley down against the last of the trees before the grassy outcrop and sat down herself alongside him.

"I guess we just make ourselves comfortable then," she said.

EPILOGUE

Lawson's eyes crept open. The sleep was ghastly; the ground was uneven. After but a few moments of lying upon the soft grass of the clearing last night, the natural lumps and bumps of the ground seemed to sharpen and dig into his ribs and hips. As his mind cleared from the sleep, he looked around at the nine others. Fleta was the only other one awake; she dabbed at her brother's forehead with a cloth.

Typical of the boy to fall ill the moment they left the town; the moment any hard work was required of them, Bronson would always find an excuse. Lawson had heard all the stories from Bark's Tavern about how Bronson would disappear for hours whenever he was supposed to help them with something, how unreliable he was…. even his Uncle Javi had bad things to say about the boy when he wasn't in earshot.

He stretched, trying to work out the kinks in

his shoulders.

Then he noticed Corin sit up, she looked over at him, regarded him with a sneer, and then rolled to stand. She stood in the camp alone, stretching to the heavens, then she shook herself free and walked into the treeline.

He saw Corin as his adversary. She was pompous, zealous and holier-than-thou; she acted as though her voice was all that mattered. He thought over their bickering from the night before and silently chuckled to himself.

Lawson knew who started the fire, and he also knew that this person would be safe so long as he could keep everyone's eyes trained on him. He saw himself as a protector, one who would happily fall upon his sword. If he had to endure the suspicion of the rest of the group, then he would.

Sitting up, he looked to the sides of him. To one side, Wendy and her adoptive sister Piper held each other in a sleepy embrace, and on the other Stokely drooled with his face pressed into the mud; he smirked at the boy, exhaling sharply from his nose. He rolled, kissed Wendy on her soft, cold cheek, then stood himself up to stretch just as Corin did moments before.

Corin was the aggressor with all the fire accusations, and he knew he had to play a game with her. Keeping all the group's eyes trained on him would involve him conflicting with Corin.

She would turn the others against him, he knew it, and that would play directly into his hands. The thing with suspicion is that the more you try to divert it, the more it centres upon you, so Lawson had a sneaky idea burning in his mind: he would confront Corin now, whilst everyone else slept. This confrontation would lay the foundation for his game of diversion.

He took off into the treeline, awkwardly shambling as he tried to activate his aching muscles. Looking around, he tried to work which direction she would choose to walk in. Luckily for him, she hadn't been sneaky about it, and the footprints pressed into the mud directed him back towards the river where they'd walked the following evening.

Lawson swept back his dark hair and wiped his face downwards as he walked. The rain from the night before had added so much moisture to his face that he seemed to sweat, even in the morning's cold.

He reached the path that they'd followed yesterday evening. On one side was the dense woodlands, and on the other, a steep scree and root covered slope, leading to the river below. He peered over the edge, down to where the water rushed.

Corin had walked down to the riverbank, and she carefully squatted at the water's edge to fill her water skin. Lawson smirked, and he stood back off the path, behind a tree to await her return. He would confront her, turn suspicion onto himself, and then the only thing he'd need to for the rest of the time they were out here, would be to drop hints, inflaming her belief now and then.

It was a good plan.

He waited for another five minutes before he spied her cresting the banking back onto the path.

"Corin," he said, startling her. She turned to face him, clutching her water skin in one hand and her Sanctuary-tree talisman in the other.

"What do you want?" she said, suspiciously.

"I think we both owe each other an apology, don't you?" he said. "For how we spoke to each other last night."

She sighed, stepping closer to him, "Lawson, I'm sorry for the way I spoke to you."

"Just the way you spoke to me? Not the words you said?" Lawson replied.

"What do you want from me?" Corin said, throwing up an arm. "If you want me to change my mind that it was you that set the fire, then you'll be left wanting. I said the words I said yesterday because I felt them. I'm sorry it got heated, I really am, but I stand by what I said."

"See, I didn't start the fire, so when you accuse me of doing that, it makes me angry," he said, lowering his eyes. "And if we have to be enemies whilst we're out here, you won't enjoy that."

"Are you threatening me?"

"Not at all," he said, stepping back, "because I know you're smart, and you'll quickly learn who you can trust out here and who you cannot."

"That's weird," she said, frowning, "you just said you weren't threatening me, and then you threatened me."

"It's not a threat," he said, focusing his gaze upon her, narrowing his eyes. "I can threaten you if that's something you want."

"No, thank you," she shook her head and then stepped to walk past him, pausing as she stood shoulder to shoulder with him. "I think it's your turn to apologise now."

"What for?" Lawson said, smirking.

"Well, did you say we both owe each other an apology?"

"Yeah, but I didn't get mine, so why would you get yours?"

"You got yours, it just wasn't exactly what you wanted." She placed the leather strap of her waterskin around her shoulders, making the skin sit snugly at her hip. Lawson grabbed the strap which lay against her back and chest, and pulled her back to face him.

"We're stepping up from threats now are we, Lawson?" she said, rolling her eyes. "You actually think that doing all of this will stop me from thinking it was you?"

"It wasn't me," he said, raising his voice, gritting his teeth for effect.

"Maybe something about The Sanctuary caused you to get angry, just like now, and you set the fire to teach it a lesson? After all, stone buildings don't respond to threats, do they?"

He turned, moving the other side of her, and pushed her against the tree he'd been leaning on. He put one hand against the tree above her shoulder, and she cowed as he pointed at her, with a grimace upon his face, "you're so perfect aren't you. You devotees are all the same; you think you're better than everyone else. Nobody else lives their lives correctly because they don't feel the same way about Inauron. I'm fucking sick of it."

"Get away from me," she said, pushing against the arm that blocked her movement back to the clearing. She looked over to her left, seeing the steepness of the banking down to the riverbed, and then turned her head right to see if she could duck beneath his arm.

"I'm telling you I didn't start the fire, and you need to look for the real firestarter instead of blaming me," Lawson said through gritted teeth.

He considered whether he was pushing too hard on her. He just wanted to ensure that she blamed him and looked no further, and he knew he wasn't supposed to actually convince her of his innocence, otherwise her attention would divert to the real culprit. It was a fine line he danced upon, like a performance in a play. He looked down at the fear in her eyes, considering whether this was the right move.

"You're scaring me," she whimpered, "get away from me."

He leaned in closer, as his final act. After this, he knew he would have to turn and walk away... he just had one more thing to say.

"Stop looking for who started the fire," he growled.

Corin pushed hard against his chest, to force him backwards, but in doing so, she slipped.

Lawson watched helplessly as he fell backwards against the path. Corin's foot slipped from under her and her body tipped down towards the steep banking. He scrambled forward to catch her, but she fell too fast. She tumbled, and her head smashed hard against a stone that jutted out of the side of the slope. Her feet tangled in the roots that matted the slippery surface and her body span, flicking the blood from her wounded head up into the air. Lawson reached out to save her, but her body flailed lifelessly down the slope until she landed, face down in the river. Even at his height, he could see the blood staining the river's water as it leaked from Corin's cracked skull.

He stood, alarmed. His limbs shook... his body wanted to reject everything he'd just seen. He frantically slid his way down the slope to her, causing rotten logs to crunch and detritus to slip, until he reached the bottom. He felt sick, and bile reached his throat - what had he done?

Bending down, Lawson attempted to lift her out of the river, but her body was caught in the tangle of roots. He unhooked her feet, and then pulled again, trying desperately to lift her. Finally, her body freed itself from the riverside and he pulled her to the bank. Her face sneered at him, involuntarily as the head wound from the rock's impact spilled blood, soaking her face. She was completely limp and wouldn't respond to any kind of stimulus. He shook her, called out to her, held her tightly in his arms, but nothing worked.

He'd killed her.

She was dead, and it was all his fault.

He just wanted to protect Stokely, but now he'd killed Corin. He stood and emptied his stomach into the river until he heaved, repeatedly with no further expulsion.

This was not how it was supposed to happen.

How could he explain this? A fire,

banishment, and then a murder? The group would turn on him, they'd exact justice for Corin's death, he knew it. He paced back and forth at the water's edge, near her lifeless body. Her eyes seemed to pierce him, so he turned away. He would need to get away. He would need to leave this place.

It was then he decided he would tell the others he wanted to go his own way, and he would leave the whole group of them to fend for themselves whilst he turned north to head for the mountains. He shook himself off and gingerly walked back up the slope, careful not to slip and share Corin's fate. When he reached the top, he looked back at the tree she'd slipped from, and the sickness attacked him once more. He dry heaved even more over the bushes besides the game trail.

Lawson wiped his face, then held his hands behind his head, interlocking his fingers, as he tried to calm his nerves. If he walked back to the camp and they could see what he'd done written all across his face; he was certain they'd exact justice upon him - a justice he knew he deserved. He took some deep breaths until his heart rate descended, then he shook himself off.

As he entered the clearing, the rest of the group were awake, and already arguing.

"Everyone's looking at me like I'm the decision-maker here. I don't know what I'm doing. I don't know where I'm going. I don't know why I'm here!" Addison yelled.

"You're the oldest," Dawn rebutted. Dawn and Addison, arguing again, as was commonplace in their relationship.

"What the fuck has that got to do with anything? Lawson is only a few weeks younger than me." Addison replied, throwing his arms in Lawson's direction.

Suddenly Lawson felt all their eyes burn into him. He gulped and steeled himself. "Hey, don't pull me into this."

He felt his face redden, his heart pound. Would they see what he'd done? Now, more than ever, he needed to get out of this clearing and leave this group behind.

"Everyone can just do what they want. If you want to stay, then stay! If you want to go, then go! I'm not the group's father; I couldn't give a shit." Addison said, conclusively.

This was Lawson's chance, he leaned over to grab his back of belongings, and threw it over his shoulder.

"I'm leaving," he said, before turning to the treeline.

"Wait," Stokely said, catching up to him. "You have to let me come with you; don't leave me with them."

"Us too," Wendy said, standing up and

helping Piper brush down her long woollen gown.

He needed to be alone; he wanted to be away from all of this, but if he argued here and stormed off, he'd bring all the unwanted attention down on him. So, he took a deep breath, and addressed his three companions.

"Fine," he said. "Let's go."

AFTERWORD

Thank you for reading my story. **If you enjoyed it, I'd very much appreciate a review or rating on the storefront your purchased it from.** It will help immensely with encouraging more readers to find my stories.

In an era of AI books generated using models trained on the intellectual property of established names, real authors' stories are at risk of becoming buried.

It's ever more difficult to find good quality writing to enjoy, so the more you praise and celebrate what you read, the more you support real authors and their efforts in keeping the written word sacred.

Add your review, today:

https://www.amazon.co.uk/dp/B0D2RKZGDT

https://www.goodreads.com/book/show/212182111-the-great-leap

Thank you again,

Dan Hanly

JOIN THE CHILDREN OF INAURON

If you enjoyed this book and would like to learn more and connect with the author, there are various communities that I would love for you to be a part of.

Connect directly with the author, share ideas, memes and connect with other fans of the series in our private Facebook Group, or Reddit community:

Facebook Group - The Children Of Inauron: https://www.facebook.com/groups/childrenofinauron/

Reddit Community - r/ChildrenOfInauron: https://www.reddit.com/r/ChildrenOfInauron/

Author's Mailing List: https://danhanly.com/

Can't wait to see you there,
Dan Hanly

ABOUT THE AUTHOR

Dan Hanly

Dan Hanly is a Welsh author of fantasy and mystery. He has a passion for telling stories in the Fantasy, Mystery and Psychological Thriller genres, and any opportunity to combine those genres is the prime place to find his works.

Explore more of Dan Hanly's works, and connect with him on his website: danhanly.com

www.ingramcontent.com/pod-product-compliance
Ingram Content Group UK Ltd.
Pitfield, Milton Keynes, MK11 3LW, UK
UKHW041505200625
6504UKWH00023B/181

9 798333 816252